Dr Ross Wyatt.

He was impossible not to notice.

Tall, with slightly wavy hair, worn just a touch too long, he didn't look like a paediatric consultant—well, whatever paediatric consultants were supposed to look like.

Some days he would be wearing jeans and a T-shirt, finished off with dark leather cowboy boots, as if he'd just got off a horse. Other days it was a smart suit, but still with a hint of rebellion. There was just something that seemed to say his muscled body wanted out of the tailored confines of the suit.

Ross Wyatt was Annika's favourite diversion, and he was certainly diverting her now.

He looked like a Spanish gypsy—just the sort of man her mother would absolutely forbid. He looked wild, untamed, thrilling.

And that smile *had* been aimed at her.

Again.

Dear Reader

A couple of years ago I wrote about two brothers from the Kolovsky family. But you don't need to have read about them to enjoy their sister Annika's story. They are a rich, fascinating family, with lots of scandal and secrets, and after two years away from them I was looking forward to visiting the Kolovsky family again—especially as I had worked out Annika's story.

I forgot that in two years people can change a lot!

Naively, I had expected to pick up where I had left off—but while I had been busy getting on with life, so too had Annika. She had grown up and made a lot of changes in the time since I last met her, and all the neat plans I had for her soon fell by the wayside!

It was fun getting to know her all over again—and working out a hero who would suit such a complex woman. I have to say—I do like her taste.

Happy reading!

Carol x

KNIGHT ON THE CHILDREN'S WARD

BY
CAROL MARINELLI

First published in Great Britain 2010
Large Print edition 2010
Harlequin Mills & Boon Limited,
Eton House, 18-24 Paradise Road,
Richmond, Surrey TW9 1SR

© Carol Marinelli 2010

ISBN: 978 0 263 21127 6

Harlequin Mills & Boon policy is to use papers that are
natural, renewable and recyclable products and made
from wood grown in sustainable forests. The logging and
manufacturing process conform to the legal environmental
regulations of the country of origin.

Printed and bound in Great Britain
by CPI Antony Rowe, Chippenham, Wiltshire

3245395 7

Carol Marinelli recently filled in a form where she was asked for her job title and was thrilled, after all these years, to be able to put down her answer as 'writer'. Then it asked what Carol did for relaxation. After chewing her pen for a moment Carol put down the truth—'writing'. The third question asked—'What are your hobbies?' Well, not wanting to look obsessed or, worse still, boring, she crossed the fingers on her free hand and answered 'swimming and tennis'. But, given that the chlorine in the pool does terrible things to her highlights, and the closest she's got to a tennis racket in the last couple of years is watching the Australian Open, I'm sure you can guess the real answer!

Carol also writes for
Mills & Boon® Modern™, where you can
find out what the Kolovskys do next in:

THE LAST KOLOVSKY PLAYBOY

Available in August 2010
from Mills & Boon® Modern™

For Helen Browne,
thank you for your friendship,
Carol x

PROLOGUE

'CAN I ask what happened, Reyes?'

Ross didn't answer his mother for a moment—instead he carried on sorting out clothes, stray earrings, books, make-up, and a shoe that didn't have a partner. He loaded them into a suitcase.

He'd been putting the job off, and when he'd finally accepted his mother's offer to sort Imelda's things, he had accepted also that with her help might come questions.

Questions that he couldn't properly answer.

'I don't know.'

'Were you arguing?' Estella asked, and then tried to hold back a sigh when Ross shook his head. 'I loved Imelda,' Estella said.

'I know,' Ross said, and that just made it harder—Imelda had loved his family and they had loved her too. 'She was funny and kind and I really, really thought I could make it work. I can't honestly think of one thing that was wrong… It was just…'

'Just what, Reyes?' His mother was the only person who called him that. When he had arrived in Australia aged seven, somehow his real name had slipped away. The other children, fascinated by the little dark-haired, olive-skinned Spanish boy who spoke no English, had translated Reyes to Ross—and that was who he had become.

Ross Wyatt.

Son of Dr George and Mrs Estella Wyatt. Older brother to Maria and Sophia Wyatt.

Only it was more complicated than that, and all too often far easier *not* to explain.

Sometimes he *had* to explain—after all, when he was growing up people had noticed the differences. George's hair, when he had had some, had been blond, like his daughters'. George was sensible, stern, perfectly nice and a wonderful father—but it wasn't his blood that ran in Ross's veins.

And he could tell from his mother's worried eyes that she was worried *that* was the problem.

Estella's brief love affair at sixteen with a forbidden Gitano, or Romany, had resulted in Reyes. The family had rallied around. His grandmother had looked after the dark baby while his mother had worked in a local bar, where, a few years later, she'd met a young Australian man, just out of medical school. George had surprised his rather staid family by falling in love and bringing home from his travels in Europe two unexpected souvenirs.

George had raised Reyes as his own, loved him as his own, and treated him no differently from his sisters.

Except Reyes, or rather Ross, *was* different.

'It wasn't…' His voice trailed off. He knew his mother was hoping for a rather more eloquent answer. He knew that she was worried just from the fact she was asking, for his mother never usually interfered. 'There wasn't that…' He couldn't find the word but he tried. He raked his mind but couldn't find it in English and so, rarely for Ross, he reverted to his native tongue. *'Buena onda.'* His mother tensed when he said it, and he knew she understood—for that was the phrase she used when she talked about his father.

His real father.

Buena onda—an attraction, a connection, a vibe from another person, from *that* person.

'Then you're looking for a fairytale, Reyes! And real-life fairytales don't have happy endings.' Estella's voice was unusually sharp. 'It's time you grew up. Look where *buena onda* left me—sixteen and pregnant.'

Only then, for the first time in his thirty-two years did Ross glimpse the anger that simmered beneath the surface of his mother.

'Passion flares and then dims. Your father—the father who held you and fed you and put you through school—stands for more than some stupid dream. Some gypsy dream that you—' She stopped abruptly, remembering perhaps that they were actually discussing him. 'Imelda was a good woman, a loyal and loving partner. She would have been a wonderful wife and you threw it away—for what?'

He didn't know.

It had been the same argument all his life as his mother and George had tried to rein in his restless energy. He struggled with conformity, though it could hardly be called rebellion.

Grade-wise he had done well at school. He had a mortgage, was a paediatrician—a consultant, in fact—he loved his family, was a good friend.

On paper all was fine.

In his soul all was not.

The mortgage wasn't for a bachelor's city dwelling— though he had a small one of those for nights on call, or when he was particularly concerned about a patient—no, his handsome wage was poured into an acreage, with stables and horses, olive and fruit trees and rows of vines, and not another residence in sight.

Just as there had been arguments about his attitude at school, even as a consultant he found it was more of the same. Budgets, policies, more budgets—all he wanted to do was his job, and at home all he wanted to do was *be*.

There was nothing wrong that he could pin down.

And there was no one who could pin him down.

Many had tried.

'Should I take this round to her?' Ross asked.

'Put it in the cupboard for now,' Estella said. 'If she comes for her things, then at least it is all together. If she doesn't…' She gave a little shrug. 'It's just some clothes. Maybe she would prefer no contact.'

He felt like a louse as he closed the zipper. Packed up two years and placed it in the cupboard.

'Imelda wanted to decorate the bedroom.' Task over, he could be a bit more honest. 'She'd done the bathroom, the spare room…' It was almost impossible to explain, but he had felt as if he were being slowly invaded. 'She said she wanted more of a commitment.'

'She cared a lot about you, Reyes...'

'I know,' he admitted. 'And I cared a lot about her.'

'It would have hurt her deeply, you ending it.'

It had. She had cried, sobbed, and then she had hit him and he'd taken it—because he deserved it, because she had almost been the one. He had hoped she was the one and then, when he could deny no longer that she wasn't... What was wrong with him?

'She loved you, Reyes!'

'So I should have just let it carry on? Married her...?'

'Of course not,' Estella said. 'But it's not just Imelda...'

It wasn't.

Imelda was one of a long line of women who had got too close—and, despite his reputation, Ross hated the pain he caused.

'I don't like it that my son hurts women.'

'I'm not getting involved with anyone for a while,' Ross said.

'You say that now...'

'I've never said it before,' Ross said. 'I mean it; I've got to sort myself out. I think I need to go back.' It took a lot of courage to look at his mum, to watch her dark eyes widen and her lips tighten. He saw the slight flinch as he said the words she had braced herself to hear for many years. 'To Spain.'

'What about your work in Russia?' Estella asked. 'All your annual leave is taken up with that. You said that it's the most important thing to you.'

It had been. As a medical student he had taken up the offer to work in a Russian orphanage on his extended summer break, with his fellow student Iosef Kolovsky. It had changed him—and now, all these years on, much of his spare time was devoted to going back. Even though Iosef was married now, and had a new baby, Ross had been determined to return to Russia later in the year. But now things had changed.

'I want to go to Spain, see my *abuelos*...' And that was a good reason to go—his grandparents were old now—but it didn't quite appease his mother. 'I'm going back next month, just for a few weeks….'

'You want to find him, don't you?'

He saw the flash of tears in her eyes and hated the pain he was causing, but his mother, whether she believed it or not, simply didn't understand.

'I want to find myself.'

CHAPTER ONE

'THERE is room for improvement, Annika.' Heather Jameson was finding this assessment particularly difficult. In most areas the student nurse was doing well. In exams, her pass-rates had been initially high, but in her second year of study they were now merely *acceptable*. In her placements it was always noted how hard she worked, and that she was well turned out, on time, but there were still a couple of issues that needed to be addressed.

'It's been noted that you're tired.' Heather cleared her throat. 'Now, I know a lot of students have to work to support themselves during their studies, but…'

Annika closed her eyes, it wouldn't enter Heather's head that she was amongst them—no, she was a Kolovsky, why on earth would *she* have to work?

Except she did—and that she couldn't reveal.

'We understand that with all your family's charity work and functions...well, that you have other balls to juggle. But, Annika, your grades are slipping—you have to find a better balance.'

'I am trying,' Annika said, but her assessment wasn't over yet.

'Annika, are you enjoying nursing?'

No.

The answer was right there, on the tip of her tongue, but she swallowed it down. For the first six months or so she had loved it—had, after so much searching, thought that she had found her vocation, a purpose to her rich and luxurious life. Despite the arguments from her mother, despite her brother Iosef's stern warning that she had no idea what she was taking on, Annika had dug in her heels and, for six months at least, she had proved everyone wrong.

The coursework had been interesting, her placements on the geriatric and palliative care wards, though scary at first, had been enjoyable, and Annika had thought she had found her passion.

But then gradually, just as Iosef had predicted it would, the joy had waned. Her surgical rotation had been a nightmare. A twenty-one-year-old had died on her shift and, sitting with the parents, Annika had felt as if she were merely playing dress-up.

It had been downhill since then.

'Have you made any friends?'

'A few,' Annika said. She tried to be friendly, tried to join in with her fellow students' chatter, tried to fit in, but the simple truth was that from the day she had started, from the day her peers had found out who she was, the family she came from, there had been an expectation, a pressure, to dazzle on the social scene. When Annika hadn't fulfilled it, they had treated her differently, and Annika had neither the confidence nor the skills to blend in.

'I know it's difficult for you, Annika…' Heather really didn't know what else to say. There was an aloofness to Annika that was hard to explain. With her thick blonde hair and striking blue eyes, and with her family's connections, one would expect her to be in constant demand, to be out-going and social, yet there was a coldness in her that had to be addressed—because it was apparent not just to staff but to the patients. 'A large part of nursing is about putting patients at ease—'

'I am always nice to the patients,' Annika inter-rupted, because she was. 'I am always polite; I introduce myself; I...' Annika's voice faded. She knew exactly what Heather was trying to say, she knew she was wooden, and she didn't know how to change it. 'I am scared of saying the wrong thing,' Annika admitted. 'I'm not good at making small talk, and I also feel very uncom-fortable when people recognize my name—when they ask questions about my family.'

'Most of the time people *are* just making small talk, not necessarily because of who you are,' Heather said, and then, when Annika's eyes drifted to the newspaper on the table, she gave a sympathetic smile, because, in Annika's case people would pry!

The Kolovsky name was famous in Melbourne.

Russian fashion designers, they created scandal and mystery and were regularly in the tabloids. Since the founder, Ivan, had died his son Aleksi had taken over the running of the business, and was causing social mayhem. There was a picture of him that very morning on page one, coming out of a casino, clearly the worse for wear, with the requisite blonde on his arm.

'Maybe nursing is not such a good idea.' Annika could feel the sting of tears behind her eyes but she would not cry. 'At the start I loved it, but lately…'

'You're a good nurse, Annika, and you could be a *very* good nurse. I'm more concerned that you're not happy. I know you're only twenty-five, but that does mean you're older than most of your group, and it's a bit harder as a mature student to fit in. Look…' She changed tack. This wasn't going the way Heather had wanted it—she was trying to bolster Annika, not have her consider quitting. 'You're starting on the children's ward today. Most of them won't have a clue about the Kolovsky name, and children are wonderful at...'

'Embarrassing you?' Annika volunteered, and managed a rare smile. 'I am dreading it.'

'I thought you might be. But children are a great leveller. I think this might be just the ward for you. Try and enjoy it, treat it as a fresh start—walk in and smile, say hello to your colleagues, open up a little, perhaps.'

'I will try.'

'And,' Heather added in a more serious tone, because she had given Annika several warnings, 'think about managing your social engagements more carefully around your roster. Request the weekends off that you need, plan more in advance.'

'I will.' Annika stood up and, unlike most other students, she shook Heather's hand.

It was little things like that, Heather thought as Annika left the room, which made her stand apart. The formal handshake, her slight Russian accent, even though she had been born in Australia. Heather skimmed through Annika's personal file, reading again that she had been home tutored, which explained a lot but not all.

There was guardedness to her, a warning that came from those blue eyes that told you to keep out.

And then occasionally, like she had just now, Annika would smile and her whole face lifted.

She was right about one thing, though, Heather thought, picking up the paper and reading about the latest antics of Annika's brother Aleksi. People did want to know more. People were fascinated by the Kolovsky family—even Heather. Feeling just a touch guilty, she read the article and wondered, not for the first time, what someone as rich and indulged as Annika was trying to prove by nursing.

There was just something about the Kolovskys.

There was still half an hour till Annika's late shift started and, rather than walk into an unfamiliar staffroom and kill time, unusually for Annika she decided to go to the canteen. She had made a sandwich at home, but bought a cup of coffee. She glanced at the tables on offer, and for perhaps the thousandth time rued her decision to work at Melbourne Bayside.

Her brother Iosef was an emergency doctor at Melbourne Central. His wife, Annie, was a nurse there too, but Iosef had been so discouraging, scathing almost, about Annika's ability that she had applied to study and work here instead. How nice it would be now to have Annie wave and ask to join her. Perhaps too it would have been easier to work in a hospital where there were already two Kolovskys—to feel normal.

'Annika!'

She felt a wash of relief as one of her fellow students waved at her. Cassie was down for the children's ward rotation too and, remembering to smile, Annika made her way over.

'Are you on a late shift?' asked Cassie.

'I am,' Annika said. 'It's my first, though. You've already done a couple of shifts there— how have you found it?'

'Awful,' Cassie admitted. 'I feel like an absolute

beginner. Everything's completely different—the drug doses, the way they do obs, and then there are the parents watching your every move.'

It sounded awful, and they sat in glum silence for a moment till Cassie spoke again. 'How was your assessment?'

'Fine,' Annika responded, and then remembered she was going to make more of an effort to be open and friendly 'Well, to tell the truth it wasn't great.'

'Oh?' Cassie blinked at the rare insight.

'My grades and things are okay; it is more to do with the way I am with my peers...' She could feel her cheeks burning at the admission. 'And with the patients too. I can be a bit stand-offish!'

'Oh!' Cassie blinked again. 'Well, if it makes you feel any better, I had my assessment on Monday. I'm to stop talking and listen more, apparently. Oh, and I'm to stop burning the candle at both ends!'

And it did make her feel better—not that Cassie hadn't fared well, more that she wasn't the only one who was struggling. Annika smiled again, but it faded when she looked up, because there, handing over some money to the cashier, *he* was.

Dr Ross Wyatt.

He was impossible not to notice.

Tall, with thick black slightly wavy hair, worn just a touch too long, he didn't look like a paediatric consultant—well, whatever paediatric consultants were supposed to look like.

Some days he would be wearing jeans and a T-shirt, finished off with dark leather cowboy boots, as if he'd just got off a horse. Other days— normally Mondays, Annika had noticed—it was a smart suit, but still with a hint of rebellion: his tie more than a little loosened, and with that silver earring he wore so well. There was just something that seemed to say his muscled, toned body wanted out of the tailored confines of his suit. And then again, but only rarely, given he wasn't a surgeon, if he'd been on call he might be wearing scrubs. Well, it almost made her dizzy: the thin cotton that accentuated the outline of his body, the extra glimpse of olive skin and the clip of Cuban-heeled boots as she'd walked behind him in the corridor one morning....

Ross Wyatt was her favourite diversion, and he was certainly diverting her now. Annika blushed as he pocketed his change, picked up his tray and caught her looking. She looked away, tried to listen to Cassie, but the slow, lazy smile he had treated her with danced before her eyes.

Always he looked good—well, not in the conventional way: her mother, Nina, would faint at his choices. Fashion was one of the rules in her family, and Ross Wyatt broke them all.

And today, on her first day on the paediatric ward, as if to welcome her, he was dressed in Annika's personal favourite and he looked divine!

Black jeans, with a thick leather belt, a black crewneck jumper that showed off to perfection his lean figure, black boots, and that silver earring. The colour was in his lips: wide, blood-red lips that curved into an easy smile. Annika hadn't got close enough yet to see his eyes, but he looked like a Spanish gypsy—just the sort of man her mother would absolutely forbid. He looked wild and untamed and thrilling—as if at any minute he would kick his heels and throw up his arms, stamp a flamenco on his way over to her. She could almost smell the smoke from the bonfire—he did that to her with a single smile…

And it was madness, Annika told herself, utter madness to be sitting in the canteen having such flights of fancy. Madness to be having such thoughts, full stop.

But just the sight of him did this.

And that smile *had been* aimed at her.

Again.

Maybe he smiled at everyone, Annika reasoned—only it didn't feel like it. Sometimes they would pass in the corridor, or she'd see him walking out of ICU, or in the canteen like this, and for a second he would stop…stop and smile.

It was as if he was waiting to know her.

And that was the other reason she was dreading

her paediatric rotation. She had once let a lift go simply because he was in it. She wanted this whole eight weeks to be over with, to be finished.

She didn't need any more distractions in an already complicated life—and Ross Wyatt would be just that: a huge distraction.

They had never spoken, never even exchanged pleasantries. He had looked as if he was going to try a couple of times, but she had scuttled back into her burrow like a frightened rabbit. Oh, she knew a little about him—he was a friend of her brother's, had been a medical student at the same time as Iosef. He still went to the orphanages in Russia, doing voluntary work during his annual leave—that was why he had been unable to attend Iosef and Annie's wedding. She had paid little attention when his name had been mentioned at the time, but since last year, when she had put his face to his name, she had yearned for snippets from her brother.

Annika swallowed as she felt the weight of his eyes still on her. She had the craziest notion that he was going to walk over and finally speak to her, so she concentrated on stirring her coffee.

'There are compensations, of course!' Cassie dragged her back to the conversation, only to voice what was already on Annika's mind. 'He's stunning, isn't he?'

'Who?' Annika flushed, stirring her coffee, but Cassie just laughed.

'Dr Drop-Dead Gorgeous Wyatt.'

'I don't know him.' Annika shrugged.

'Well, he's looking right over at you!' Cassie sighed. 'He's amazing, and the kids just love him—he really is great with them.'

'How?'

'I don't know...' Cassie admitted. 'He just...' She gave a frustrated shrug. 'He *gets* them, I guess. He just seems to understand kids, puts them at ease.'

Annika did not, would not, look over to where he sat, but sometimes she was sure he looked over to her—because every now and then she felt her skin warm. Every now and then it seemed too complicated to move the sandwich from her hand up to her mouth.

Ross Wyatt certainly didn't put Annika at ease.

He made her awkward.

He made her aware.

Even walking over to empty out her tray and head to work she felt as if her movements were being noted, but, though it was acutely awkward, somehow she liked the feeling he evoked. Liked the thrill in the pit of her stomach, the rush that came whenever their paths briefly crossed.

As she sat in handover, listening to the list of patients and their ages and diagnoses, he popped his head around the door to check something with Caroline, the charge nurse, and Annika felt a dull blush on her neck as she heard his voice properly for the first time.

Oh, she'd heard him laugh on occasion, and heard his low tones briefly as they'd passed in the corridor when he was talking with a colleague, but she'd never fully heard him speak.

And as he spoke now, about an order for pethidine, Annika found out that toes did curl—quite literally!

His voice was rich and low and without arrogance. He'd made Caroline laugh with something he said—only Annika couldn't properly process it, because instead she was feeling her toes bunch up inside her sensible navy shoes.

'Back to Luke Winters...'

As the door closed so too did her mind on Ross, and she began concentrating carefully on the handover, because this rotation she *had* to do well.

'He's fifteen years old, Type 1 Diabetes, non-compliant...'

Luke Winters, Annika learnt, was causing not just his family but the staff of the children's ward a lot of problems.

It was his third admission in twelve months. He was refusing to take his insulin at times, ignoring his diet, and he had again gone into DKA—a dangerous, toxic state that could kill. He had an ulcer on his leg that had been discovered on admission, though had probably been there for some time. It would take a long time to heal and might require a skin graft. His mother was frantic—Luke had come to the ward from ICU two days ago and was causing chaos. His room was a mess, and he had told the domestic this morning, none too politely, to get out.

He was now demanding that his catheter be removed, and basically both the other patients and the staff wanted him taken to an adult ward, though Ross Wyatt was resisting.

'"Teenagers, even teenagers who think they are adults, are still children."' Caroline rolled her eyes. 'His words, not mine. Anyway, Luke's mum is at work and not due in till this evening. Hopefully we can have some order by then. Okay…' She stared at the patient sheet and allocated the staff, pausing when she came to Annika. 'I might put you in cots with Amanda…' She hesitated. 'But you haven't been in cots yet, have you, Cassie?'

When Cassie shook her head and Caroline changed her allocation Annika felt a flood of relief—she had never so much as held a baby, and the thought of looking after a sick one petrified her.

'Annika, perhaps you could have beds eight to sixteen instead—though given it's your first day don't worry about room fifteen.'

'Luke?' Annika checked, and Caroline nodded.

'I don't want to scare you off on your first day.'

'He won't scare me,' Annika said. Moody teenagers she could deal with; it was babies and toddlers that scared her.

'His room needs to be sorted.'

'It will be.'

'Okay!' Caroline smiled. 'If you're sure? Good luck.'

Lisa, who was in charge of Annika's patients, showed her around the ward. It was, as Cassie had said, completely different. Brightly painted, with a detailed mural running the length of the corridor, and divided pretty much into three.

There were cots for the littlest patients—two

large rooms, each containing four cots. Then there were eight side rooms that would house a cot or a bed, depending on the patient's age. Finally there were three large four-bedded rooms, filled with children of various ages.

'Though we do try to keep ages similar,' Lisa said, 'sometimes it's just not possible.' She pointed out the crash trolley, the drug room, and two treatment rooms. 'We try to bring the children down here for dressings and IV's and things like that.'

'So they don't upset the other children?' Annika checked.

'That, and also, even if they are in a side room, it's better they have anything unpleasant done away from their bed. Obviously if they're infectious we can't bring them down, but generally we try to do things away from the bedside.'

Annika was offered a tabard to replace her navy one. She had a choice of aprons, all brightly coloured and emblazoned with cartoon characters, and though her first instinct was to politely decline, she remembered she was making an

effort, so chose a red one, with fish and mer-
maids on it. She felt, as she slipped it over her
head, utterly stupid.

Annika started with the obs. Lunches were
being cleared away, and the ward was being
readied for afternoon rest-time.

The children eyed her suspiciously—she was
new and they knew it.

'What's that for?' A mother demanded angrily
as her first patient burst into tears when Annika
went to wrap a blood pressure cuff around her
arm.

Lisa moved quickly to stop her.

'We don't routinely do blood pressure,' Lisa
said, showing her the obs form. 'Unless it's
stated on the chart.'

'Okay.'

'Just pulse, temp and respirations.'

'Thank you.'

The little girl wouldn't stop crying. In fact she
shrieked every time Annika tried to venture near,
so Lisa quickly took her temperature as Annika
did the rest of the obs. In the room, eight sets

of eyes watched her every awkward move: four from the patients, four from their mothers.

'Can I have a drink?' a little boy asked.

'Of course,' Annika said, because that was easy. She checked his chart and saw that he was to be encouraged to take fluids. 'Would you like juice or milk…?'

'He's lactose intolerant!' his mother jumped in. 'It says so above his bed.'

'Always look at the whiteboard above the bed,' Lisa said. 'And it will say in his admission slip too, which is clipped to his folder.'

'Of course.' Annika fled to the kitchen, where Cassie was warming a bottle.

'Told you!' Cassie grinned when Annika told her all that had happened. 'It's like landing on Mars!'

But she wasn't remotely nervous about a sullen Luke. She knew he had no relatives with him, and was glad to escape the suspicious eyes of parents. It was only when she went into the side ward and realised that Ross was in there, talking, that she felt flustered.

'I can come back.'

'No.' He smiled. 'We're just having a chat, and Luke needs his obs done.'

'I don't want them done,' Luke snarled as she approached the bed.

That didn't ruffle her either—her extra shifts at the nursing home had taught her well, because belligerence was an everyday occurrence there!

'I will come back in five minutes, then,' Annika said, just as she would say to Cecil, or Elsie, or any of the oldies who refused to have their morning shower.

'I won't want them done then either.'

'Then I will come back five minutes later, and five minutes after that again. My name is Annika; it would seem that you'll be seeing a lot of me this afternoon.' She gave him a smile. 'Every five minutes, in fact.'

'Just take them now, then.'

So she did.

Annika made no attempt at small talk. Luke clearly didn't want it, and anyway Ross was talking to him, telling him that there was no question of him going home, that he was still extremely ill and would be here for a few weeks—at least until the ulcer on his leg was healed and he was compliant with his medication. Yes, he would take the catheter out, so long as Luke agreed to wee into a bottle so that they could monitor his output.

Luke begrudgingly agreed to that.

And then Ross told him that the way he had spoken to the cleaner that morning was completely unacceptable.

'You can be as angry as you like, Luke, but it's not okay to be mean.'

'So send me home, then.'

'That's not going to happen.'

Annika wrote down his obs, which were all fine, and then, as Ross leant against the wall and Luke lay on the bed with his eyes closed, she spoke.

'When the doctor has finished talking to you I will come back and sort out your room.'

'And I'll tell *you* the same thing I said to the cleaner.'

She saw Ross open his mouth to intervene as Luke snarled at her, but in this Annika didn't need his help.

'Would you rather I waited till children's nap-time is over?' Annika asked. 'When you feel a little less grumpy.'

'Ha-ha...' he sneered, and then he opened his eyes and gave a nasty sarcastic grin. 'Nice apron!'

'I hate it,' she said. 'Wearing it is a bit de-moralising and...' She thought for a moment as Luke just stared. 'Well, I find it a bit patronising really. If I were in cots it would maybe be appropriate. Still...' Annika shrugged. 'Sometimes we have to do things we don't want to.' She replaced his chart. 'I'll be back to clean your room shortly.'

Ross was at the nurses' station writing notes when she came over after completing the rest of the obs. He grinned when he saw her.

'Nice apron.'

'It's growing on me!' Annika said. 'Tomorrow I want to wear the one with robots!'

'I can't wait!' he replied, and, oh, for a witty retort—but there wasn't one forthcoming, so instead she asked Lisa where the cleaning cupboard was and found a bin liner. She escaped to the rather more soothing, at least for Annika, confines of Luke's room.

It was disgusting.

In the short time he had been in the room he had accumulated cups and plates and spilt drinks. There were used tissues on the floor. His bed was a disgrace because he refused to let anyone tidy it, and there were loads of cards from friends, along with all the gadgets fifteen-year-olds seemed to amass.

Luke didn't tell her to leave—probably because he sensed she wouldn't care if he did.

Annika was used to moods.

She had grown up surrounded by them and had chosen to completely ignore them.

Her father's temper had been appalling, though

it had never been aimed towards her—she had been the apple of his eye. Her brothers were dark and brooding, and her mother could sulk for Russia.

A fifteen-year-old was nothing, *nothing*, compared to that lot.

Luke ignored her.

Which was fine by Annika.

'Everything okay?' Lisa checked as she finally headed to the kitchen with a trolley full of used plates and cups.

'All's fine.' The ward was quiet, the lights all dimmed, and Ross was still at the desk. 'Do you need me to do anything else, or is it okay if I carry on with Luke's room?'

'Please do,' Lisa said.

Luke wasn't ignoring her now—instead he watched as she sorted out his stuff into neat piles and put some of it into a bag.

'Your mum can take these home to wash.'

Other stuff she put into drawers.

Then she tacked some cards to the wall. All that was messy now, Annika decided as she wiped down the surfaces in his room, was the patient and his bed.

'Now your catheter is out it will be easier to have a shower. I can run it for you.'

He said neither yes nor no, so Annika headed down the ward and found the linen trolley, selected some towels and then found the showers. She worked out the taps and headed back to her patient, who was a bit wobbly but refused a wheelchair.

'Take my arm, then.'

'I can manage,' Luke said, and he said it again when she tried to help him undress.

'You have a drip...'

'I'm not stupid; I've had a drip before.'

Okay!

So she left him to it, and she didn't hover outside, asking if he was okay every two minutes, because that would have driven Luke insane. Instead she moved to the other end of the bathroom, so she could hear him if he called, and checked her reflection, noting the huge smudges under her eyes, which her mother would point out to her when she went there for dinner at the weekend.

She was exhausted. Annika rested her head against the mirror for a moment and just wanted to close her eyes and sleep. She was beyond exhausted, in fact, and from this morning's assessment it seemed it had been noticed.

Heather would never believe that she was working shifts in a nursing home, and the hardest slots too—five a.m. till eight a.m. if she was on a late shift at the hospital, and seven p.m. till ten p.m. if she was on an early. Oh, and a couple of nights shifts on her days off.

She was so tired. Not just bone-tired, but tired of arguing, tired of being told to pack in nursing, to come home, to be sensible, tired of being told that she didn't need to nurse—she was a Kolovsky.

'Iosef is a doctor,' Annika had pointed out.

'Iosef is a fool,' her mother had said, 'and as for that slut of a wife of his...'

'Finished.'

She was too glum thinking about her mother

to smile and cheer as Luke came out, in fresh track pants and with his hair dripping wet.

'You smell much better,' Annika settled for instead, and the shower must have drained Luke because he let Annika thread his T-shirt through his IV.

'What are you looking so miserable about?' Luke asked.

'Stuff,' Annika said.

'Yeah,' Luke said, and she was rewarded with a smile from him.

'Oh, that's *much* better!' Lisa said, popping her head into the bathroom. 'You're looking very handsome.' Annika caught Luke's eyes and had to stop herself from rolling her own. She sort of understood him—she didn't know how, she just did. 'Your mum's here, by the way!' Lisa added.

'Great,' Luke muttered as Annika walked him back. 'That's all I need. You haven't met her yet...'

'You haven't met mine!' Annika said, and they both smiled this time—a real smile.

Annika surprised herself, because rarely, if ever, did she speak about her family, and especially not to a patient. But they had a little giggle as they walked, and she was too busy concentrating on Luke and pushing his IV to notice Ross look up from the desk and watch the unlikely new friends go by.

'Are you still here?' Caroline frowned, quite a long time later, because, as pedantic as Ross was, consultants didn't usually hang around all day.

'I just thought I'd catch up on some paperwork.'

'Haven't you got an office to go to?' she teased.

He did, but for once he didn't have that much paperwork to do.

'Annika!' Caroline called her over from where Annika was stacking the linen trolley after returning from her supper break. 'Come and get started on your notes. I'll show you how we do them. It's different to the main wards.'

He didn't look up, but he smelt her as she came around the desk.

A heavy, musky fragrance perfumed the air, and though he wrote it maybe twenty times a day, he had misspelled *diarrhoea*, and Ross frowned at his spiky black handwriting, because the familiar word looked completely wrong.

'Are you wearing perfume, Annika?' He didn't look up at Caroline's stern tone.

'A little,' Annika said, because she'd freshened up after her break.

'You can't wear perfume on the children's ward!' Caroline's voice had a familiar ring to it—one Ross had heard all his life.

'What do you mean—you just didn't want to go to school? You can't wear an earring. You just have to, that's all. You just don't. You just can't.'

'Go and wash it off,' Caroline said, and now Ross did look up. He saw her standing there, wary, tight-lipped, in that ridiculous apron. 'There are children with allergies, asthma. You just *can't* wear perfume, Annika—didn't you think?'

Caroline was right, Ross conceded, there were children with allergies and, as much as he liked it, Kolovsky musk post-op might be a little bit too much, but he wanted to step in, wanted to grin at Annika and tell her she smelt divine, tell her *not* to wash it off, for her to tell Caroline that she wouldn't.

And he knew that she was thinking it too!

It was a second, a mere split second, but he saw her waver—and Ross had a bizarre feeling that she was going to dive into her bag for the bottle and run around the ward, ripping off her apron and spraying perfume. The thought made him smile—at the wrong moment, though, because Annika saw him and, although Ross snapped his face to bland, she must have thought he was enjoying her discomfort.

Oh, but he wanted to correct her.

He wanted to follow her and tell her that wasn't what he'd meant as she duly turned around and headed for the washroom.

He wanted to apologise when she came back unscented and sat at her stool while Caroline nit-picked her way through the nursing notes.

Instead he returned to his own notes.

DIAOR… He scrawled a line through it again.

Still her fragrance lingered.

He got up without a word and, unusually for Ross, closed his office door. Then he picked up his pen and forced himself to concentrate.

DIARREA.

He hurled his pen down. Who cared anyway? They knew what he meant!

He was not going to fancy her, nor, if he could help it, even talk much to her.

He was off women.

He had sworn off women.

And a student nurse on his ward—well, it couldn't be without complications.

She was his friend's little sister too.

No way!

Absolutely not.

He picked up his pen and resumed his notes.

'*The baby has*,' he wrote instead, '*severe gastroenteritis.*'

CHAPTER TWO

HE DID a very good job of ignoring her.

He did an excellent job at pulling rank and completely speaking over her head, or looking at a child or a chart or the wall when he had no choice but to address her. And at his student lecture on Monday he paid her no more attention than any of the others. He delivered a talk on gastroenteritis, and, though he hesitated as he went to spell *diarrhoea*, he wrote it up correctly on the whiteboard.

She, Ross noted, was ignoring him too. She asked no questions at the end of the lecture, but an annoying student called Cassie made up for that.

Once their eyes met, but she quickly flicked hers away, and he, though he tried to discount it, saw the flush of red on her neck and wished that he hadn't.

Yes, he did a very good job at ignoring her and not talking to her till, chatting to the pathologist in the bowels of the hospital a few days later, he glanced up at the big mirror that gave a view around the corridor and there was Annika. She was yawning, holding some blood samples, completely unaware she was being watched.

'I've been waiting for these...' Ross said when she turned the corner, and she jumped slightly at the sight of him. He took the bloodwork and stared at the forms rather than at her.

'The chute isn't working,' Annika explained. 'I said I'd drop them in on my way home.'

'I forgot to sign the form.'

'Oh.'

He would rather have taken ages to sign the form, but the pathologist decided they had been talking for too long and hurried him along. Annika had stopped for a moment to put on her jacket, and as his legs were much longer than hers somehow, despite trying not to, he had almost caught her up as they approached the flapping black plastic doors. It would have been really rude had she not held it open—and just plain wrong for him not to thank her and fall into step beside her.

'You look tired,' Ross commented.

'It's been a long shift.'

This had got them halfway along the corridor, and now they should just walk along in silence, Ross reasoned. He was a consultant, and he could be as rude and as aloof as he liked—except he could hear his boots, her shoes, and an endless, awful silence. It was Ross who filled it.

'I've actually been meaning to talk to you...' He had—long before he had liked her.

'Oh?' She felt the adrenaline kick in, the effect of him close up far more devastating than his smile, and yet she liked it. She liked it so much that she slowed down her pace and looked over to him. 'About what?'

She could almost smell the bonfire—all those smiles, all that guessing, all that waiting was to be put to rest now they were finally talking.

'I know your brother Iosef,' Ross said. 'He

asked me to keep an eye out for you when you started.'

'Did he?' Her cheeks were burning, the back of her nose was stinging, and she wanted to run, to kick up her heels and run from him—because all the time she'd thought it was her, not her family, that he saw.

'I've always meant to introduce myself. Iosef is a good friend.' It was her jacket's fault, Ross decided. Her jacket smelt of the forbidden perfume. It smelt so much of her that he forgot, for a second, his newly laid-down rules. 'We should catch up some time...'

'Why?' She turned very blue eyes to him. 'So that you can report back to Iosef?'

'Of course not.'

'Tell him I'm doing fine,' Annika snapped, and, no, she didn't kick up her heels, and she didn't run, but she did walk swiftly away from him.

A year.

For more than a year she'd carried a torch, had secretly hoped that his smile, those looks they had shared, had meant something. All that time she had thought it had been about her, and yet again it wasn't.

Again, all she was was a Kolovsky.

It rankled. On the drive home it gnawed and burnt, but when she got there her mother had left a long message on the answer machine which rankled rather more.

They needed to go over details, she reminded her daughter.

It was the charity ball in just three weeks—as if Annika could ever forget.

When Annika had been a child it had been discovered that her father had an illegitimate son— one who was being raised in an orphanage in Russia.

Levander had been brought over to Australia. Her father had done everything to make up for the wretched years his son had suffered, and Levander's appalling early life had been kept a closely guarded family secret.

Now, though, the truth was starting to seep

out. And Nina, anticipating a public backlash, had moved into pre-emptive damage control.

Huge donations had been sent to several orphanages, and to a couple of street-kid pro-grammes too.

And then there was *The Ball.*

It was to be a dazzling, glitzy affair they would all attend. Levander was to be excused because he was in England, but the rest of the family would be there. Iosef and his wife, her brother Aleksi, and of course Annika. They would all look glossy and beautiful and be photographed to the max, so that when the truth inevitably came out the spin doctors would be ready.

Already were ready.

Annika had read the draft of the waiting press release.

The revelation of his son Levander's suf-fering sent Ivan Kolovsky to an early grave. He was thrilled when his second-born, Iosef, on qualifying as a doctor, chose to work amongst the poor in Russia, and Ivan would be proud to know that his daughter, Annika, is now studying nursing. On Ivan's deathbed he begged his wife to set up the Kolovsky Foundation, which has gone on to raise huge amounts (insert current figure).

Lies.

Lies based on twisted truths. And only since her father's death had Annika started to question them.

And now she had, everything had fallen apart.

Her mother had never hit her before—oh, maybe a slap on the leg when she was little and had refused to converse in Russian, and once as a teenager, when her mother had found out she was eating burgers on her morning jog, Annika had nursed a red cheek and a swollen eye...but hardly anything major...

Until she had asked about Levander.

They had been sorting out her father's things, a painful task at the best of times, and Annika had come across some letters. She hadn't read them—she hadn't had a chance to. Nina had snatched them out of her hands, but Annika had asked her mother a question that had been nagging. It was a question her brothers had refused to answer when she had approached them with it. She asked whether Ivan and Nina had known that Levander was in an orphanage all those years.

Her mother had slapped her with a viciousness that had left Annika reeling—not at the pain but with shock.

She had then discovered that when she started to think, to suggest, to question, to find her own path in life, the love and support Annika had thought was unconditional had been pulled up like a drawbridge.

And the money had been taken away too.

Annika deleted her mother's message and prepared a light supper. She showered, and then, because she hadn't had time to this morning, ironed her white agency nurse's uniform and dressed. Tying her hair back, she clipped on her name badge.

Annika Kolovsky.

No matter how she resisted, it was who she was—and *all* she was to others.

She should surely be used to it by now.

Except she'd thought Ross had seen something else—thought for a foolish moment that Ross Wyatt had seen her for herself. Yet again it came back to one thing.

She was a Kolovsky.

CHAPTER THREE

'SLEEP well, Elsie.' Elsie didn't answer as Annika tucked the blankets round the bony shoulders of the elderly lady.

Elsie had spat out her tablets and thrown her dinner on the floor. She had resisted at every step of Annika undressing her and getting her into bed. But now that she was in bed she relaxed, especially when Annika positioned the photo of her late husband, Bertie, where the old lady could see him.

'I'll see you in the morning. I have another shift then.'

Still Elsie didn't answer, and Annika wished she would. She loved the stories Elsie told, during the times when she was lucid. But Elsie's confusion had worsened because of an infection, and she had been distressed tonight, resenting any intrusion. Nursing patients with dementia was often a thankless task, and Annika's shifts exhausted her, but at least, unlike on the children's ward, where she had been for a week now, here Annika knew what she was doing.

Oh, it was back-breaking, and mainly just sheer hard work, but she had been here for over a year now, and knew the residents. The staff of the private nursing home had been wary at first, but they were used to Annika now. She had proved herself a hard worker and, frankly, with a skeleton staff, so long as the patients were clean and dry, and bedded at night or dressed in the morning, nobody really cared who she was or why someone as rich as Annika always put her hand up for extra shifts.

It was ridiculous, though.

Annika knew that.

In fact she was ashamed that she stood in the forecourt of a garage next to a filthy old ute and had to pre-pay twenty dollars, because that was all she had until her pay from the nursing home went in tomorrow, to fill up the tank of a six-figure powder-blue sports car.

It had been her twenty-first birthday present.

Her mother had been about to upgrade it when Annika had declared she wanted to study nursing, and when she had refused to give in the financial plug had been pulled.

Her car now needed a service, which she couldn't afford. The sensible thing, of course, would be to sell it—except, despite its being a present, technically, it didn't belong to her: it was a company car.

So deep in thought was Annika, so bone-weary from a day on the children's ward and a twilight shift at the nursing home, that she didn't notice the man crossing the forecourt towards her.

'Annika?' He was putting money in his wallet. He had obviously just paid, and she glanced around rather than look at him. She was one burning blush, and not just because it was Ross, but rather because someone from work had seen her. She had done a full shift on the children's ward, and was due back there at midday tomorrow, so there was no way on earth she should be cramming in an extra shift, but she clearly was—two, actually, not that he could know! The white agency nurse dress seemed to glow under the fluorescent lights.

He could have nodded and left it there.

He damn well *should* nod and leave it there— and maybe even have a quiet word with Caroline tomorrow, or Iosef, perhaps.

Or say nothing at all—just simply forget.

He chose none of the above.

'How about a coffee?'

'It's late.'

'I know it's late,' Ross said, 'but I'm sure you could use a coffee. There's an all-night cafe a kilometre up the road—I'll see you there.'

She nearly didn't go.

She was *extremely* tempted not to go. But she had no choice.

Normally she was careful about being seen in her agency uniform, but she didn't have her jacket in the car, and she'd been so low on petrol...

Anyway, Annika told herself, it was hardly a crime—all her friends did agency shifts. How the hell would a student survive otherwise?

His grim face told her her argument would be wasted.

'I know students have to work...' he had bought her a coffee and she added two sugars '...and I know it's probably none of my business...'

'It *is* none of your business,' Annika said.

'But I've heard Caroline commenting, and I've seen you yawning...' Ross said. 'You look like you've got two black eyes.'

'So tell Caroline—or report back to my brother.' Annika shrugged. 'Then your duty is done.'

'Annika!' Ross was direct. 'Do you go out of your way to be rude?'

'Rude?'

'I'm trying *not* to talk to Caroline; I'm trying to talk to *you*.'

'Check up on me, you mean, so that Iosef—'

He whistled in indignation. 'This has nothing to do with your brother. It's my ward, Annika.

You were on an early today; you're on again tomorrow...'

'How do you know?'

'Sorry?'

'My shift tomorrow. How do you know?'

And that he couldn't answer—but the beat of silence did.

He'd checked.

Not deliberately—he hadn't swiped keys and found the nursing roster—but as he'd left the ward he had glanced up at the whiteboard and seen that she was on tomorrow.

He had noted to himself that she was on tomorrow.

'I saw the whiteboard.'

And she could have sworn that he blushed. Oh, his cheeks didn't flare like a match to a gas ring, as Annika's did—he was far too laid-back for that, and his skin was so much darker—but there was something that told her he was embarrassed. He blinked, and then his lips twitched in a very short smile, and then he blinked again. There was no colour as such to his eyes—in fact they were blacker than black, so much so that she couldn't even make out his pupils. He was staring, and so was she. They were sitting in an all-night coffee shop. She was in her uniform and he was telling her off for working, and yet she was sure there was more.

Almost sure.

'So, Iosef told you to keep an eye out for me?' she said, though more for her own benefit—that smile wouldn't fool her again.

'He said that he was worried about you, that you'd pretty much cut yourself off from your family.'

'I haven't,' Annika said, and normally that would have been it. Everything that was said stayed in the family, but Ross was Iosef's friend and she was quite sure he knew more. 'I see my mother each week; I am attending a family charity ball soon. Iosef and I argued, but only because he thinks I'm just playing at nursing.'

This wasn't news to Ross. Iosef had told him many things—how Annika was spoilt, how she stuck at nothing, how nursing was her latest flight of fancy. Of course Ross could not say this, so he just sat as she continued.

'I have not cut myself off from my family. Aleksi and I are close...' She saw his jaw tighten, as everyone's did these days when her brother's name was mentioned. Aleksi was trouble. Aleksi, now head of the Kolovsky fortune, was a loose cannon about to explode at any moment. Annika was the only one he was close to; even his twin Iosef was being pushed aside as Aleksi careered out of control. She looked down at her coffee then, but it blurred, so she pressed her fingers into her eyes.

'You *can* talk to me,' Ross said.

'Why would I?'

'Because that's what people do,' Ross said. 'Some people you know you can talk to, and some people...' He stopped then. He could see she didn't understand, and neither really did Ross. He swallowed down the words he had been about to utter and changed tack. 'I am going to Spain in three, nearly four weeks.' He smiled at her frown. 'Caroline doesn't know; Admin doesn't know. In truth, they are going to be furious when they find out. I am putting off telling them till I have spoken with a friend who I am hoping can cover for me...'

'Why are you telling me this?'

'Because I'm asking you to tell *me* things you'd rather no one else knew.'

She took her fingers out of her eyes and looked up to find *that* smile.

'It would be rude not to share,' he said.

He *was* dangerous.

She could almost hear her mother's rule that you discussed family with no one breaking.

'My mother does not want me to nurse,' Annika tentatively explained. And the skies didn't open with a roar, missiles didn't engage. There was just the smell of coffee and the warmth of his eyes. 'She has cut me off financially until I come back home. I still see her, I still go over and I still attend functions. I haven't cut myself off. It is my mother who has cut me off—financially, anyway. That's why I'm working these shifts.'

He didn't understand—actually, he didn't fully believe it.

He could guess at what her car was worth, and he knew from his friend that Annika was doted upon. Then there was Aleksi and his billions, and Iosef, even if they argued, would surely help her out.

'Does Iosef know you're doing extra shifts?'

'We don't talk much,' Annika admitted. 'We don't get on; we just never have. I was always a daddy's girl, the little princess… Levander, my older brother, thinks the same…' She gave a helpless shrug. 'I was always pleading with them to toe the line, to stop making waves in the family. Iosef is just waiting for me to quit.'

'Iosef cares about you.'

'He offers me money,' Annika scoffed. 'But really he is just waiting for this phase to be over. If I want money I will ask Aleksi, but, really, how can I be independent if all I do is cash cheques?'

'And how can you study and do placements

and be a Kolovsky if you're cramming in extra shifts everywhere?'

She didn't know how, because she was failing at every turn.

'I get by,' she settled for. 'I have learnt that I can blowdry my own hair, that foils every month are not essential, that a massage each week and a pedicure and manicure...' Her voice sounded strangled for a moment. 'I am spoilt, as my brothers have always pointed out, and I am trying to learn not to be, but I keep messing up.'

'Tell me?'

She was surprised when she opened her screwed up eyes, to see that he was smiling.

'Tell me how you mess up?'

'I used to eat a lot of takeaway,' she admitted, and he was still smiling, so she was more honest, and Ross found out that Annika's idea of takeaway wasn't the same as his! 'I had the restaurants deliver.'

'Can't you cook?'

'I'm a fantastic cook,' Annika answered.

'That's right.' Ross grinned. 'I remember Iosef saying you were training as a pastry chef…in Paris?' he checked.

'I was only there six months.' Annika wrinkled her nose. 'I had given up on modelling and I so badly wanted to go. It took me two days to realise I had made a mistake, and then six months to pluck up the courage to admit defeat. I had made such a fuss, begged to go… Like I did for nursing.'

He didn't understand.

He thought of his own parents—if he'd said that he wanted to study life on Mars they'd have supported him. But then he'd always known what he wanted to do. Maybe if one year it had been Mars, the next Venus and then Pluto, they'd have decided otherwise. Maybe this was tough love that her mother thought she needed to prove that nursing was what she truly wanted to do.

'So you can cook?' It was easier to change the subject.

'Gourmet meals, the most amazing desserts,

but a simple dinner for one beats me every time...' She gave a tight shrug. 'But I'm slowly learning.'

'How else have you messed up?'

She couldn't tell him, but he was still smiling, so maybe she could.

'I had a credit card,' she said. 'I have always had one, but I just sent the bill to our accountants each month...'

'Not now?'

'No.'

Her voice was low and throaty, and Ross found himself leaning forward to catch it.

'It took me three months to work out that they weren't settling it, and I am still paying off that mistake.'

'But you love nursing?' Ross said, and then frowned when she shook her head.

'I don't know,' Annika admitted. 'Sometimes I don't even know why I am doing this. It's the same as when I wanted to be a pastry chef, and then I did jewellery design—that was a mistake too.'

'Do you think you've made a mistake with nursing?' Ross asked.

Annika gave a tight shrug and then shook her head—he was hardly the person to voice her fears to.

'You can talk to me, Annika. You can trust that it won't—'

'Trust?' She gave him a wide-eyed look. 'Why would I trust you?'

It was the strangest answer, and one he wasn't expecting. Yet why should she trust him? Ross pondered. All he knew was that she could.

'You need to get home and get some rest,' Ross settled for—except he couldn't quite leave it there. 'How about dinner...?'

And this was where every woman jumped, this was where Ross always kicked himself and told himself to slow down, because normally they never made it to dinner. Normally, about an hour from now, they were pinning the breakfast menu on the nearest hotel door or hot-footing it back to his city abode—only this was Annika, who instead drained her coffee and stood up.

'No, thank you. It would make things difficult at work.'

'It would,' Ross agreed, glad that one of them at least was being sensible.

'Can I ask that you don't tell Caroline or anyone about this?'

'Can I ask that you save these shifts for your days off, or during your holidays?'

'No.'

They walked out to the car park, to his dusty ute and her powder-blue car. Ross was relaxed and at ease, Annika a ball of tension, so much so that she jumped at the bleep of her keys as she unlocked the car.

'I'm not going to say anything to Caroline.'

'Thank you.'

'Just be careful, okay?'

'I will.'

'You can't mess up on any ward, but especially not on children's.'

'I won't,' Annika said. 'I don't. I am always so, so careful…' And she was. Her brain hurt because she was so careful, pedantic, and always,

always checked. Sometimes it would be easier not to care so.

'Go home and go to bed,' Ross said. 'Will you be okay to drive?'

'Of course.'

He didn't want her to drive; he wanted to bundle her into his ute and take her back to the farm, or head back into the coffee shop and talk till three a.m., or, maybe just kiss her?

Except he was being sensible now.

'Night, then,' he said.

'Goodnight.'

Except neither of them moved.

'Why are you going to Spain?' Unusually, it was Annika who broke the silence.

'To sort out a few things.'

'I'm staying here for a few weeks,' Annika said, with just a hint of a smile. 'To sort out a few things.'

'It will be nice,' Ross said, 'when things are a bit more sorted.'

'Very nice,' Annika agreed, and wished him goodnight again.

'If you change your mind...' He snapped his mouth closed; he really mustn't go there.

Annika was struggling. She didn't want to get into her car. She wanted to climb into the ute with him, to forget about sorting things out for a little while. She wanted him to drive her somewhere secluded. She wanted the passion those black eyes promised, wanted out of being staid, and wanted to dive into recklessness.

'Drive carefully.'

'You too.'

They were talking normally—extremely politely, actually—yet their minds were wandering off to dangerous places: lovely, lovely places that there could be no coming back from.

'Go,' Ross said, and she felt as if he were kissing her. His eyes certainly were, and her body felt as if he were.

She was shaking as she got in the car, and the key was too slim for the slot. She had to make herself think, had to slow her mind down and turn on the lights and then the ignition.

He was beside her at the traffic lights. Ross

was indicating right for the turn to the country; Annika aimed straight for the city.

It took all her strength to go straight on.

CHAPTER FOUR

ELSIE frowned from her pillow when Annika awoke her a week later at six a.m. with a smile.

'What are you so cheerful about?' Elsie asked dubiously. She often lived in the past, but sometimes in the morning she clicked to the present, and those were the mornings Annika loved best.

She recognised Annika—oh, not all of the time, sometimes she spat and swore at the intrusion, but some mornings she was Elsie, with beady eyes and a generous glimpse of a once sharp mind.

'I just am.'

'How's the children's ward?' Elsie asked. Clearly even in that fog-like existence she mainly inhabited somehow she heard the words Annika said, even if she didn't appear to at the time.

Annika was especially nice to Elsie. Well, she was nice to all the oldies, but Elsie melted her heart. The old lady had shrunk to four feet tall and there was more fat on a chip. She swore, she spat, she growled, and every now and then she smiled. Annika couldn't help but spoil her, and sometimes it annoyed the other staff, because many showers had to be done before the day shift appeared, and there really wasn't time to make drinks, but Elsie loved to have a cup of milky tea before she even thought about moving and Annika always made her one. The old lady sipped on it noisily as Annika sorted out her clothes for the day.

'It's different on the children's ward,' Annika said. 'I'm not sure if I like it.'

'Well, if it isn't work that's making you cheerful then I want to know what is. It has to be a man.'

'I'm just in a good mood.'

'It's a man,' Elsie said. 'What's his name?'

'I'm not saying.'

'Why not? I tell you about Bertie.'

This was certainly true!

'Ross.' Annika helped her onto the shower chair. 'And that's all I'm saying.'

'Are you courting?'

Annika grinned at the old-fashioned word.

'No,' Annika said.

'Has he asked you out?'

'Sort of,' Annika said as she wheeled her down to the showers. 'Just for dinner, but I said no.'

'So you're just flirting, then!' Elsie beamed. 'Oh, you lucky, lucky girl. I loved flirting.'

'We're not flirting, Elsie,' Annika said. 'In fact we're now ignoring each other.'

'Why would you do that?'

'Just leave it, Elsie.'

'Flirt!' Elsie insisted as Annika pulled her nightgown over her head. 'Ask him out.'

'Enough, Elsie,' Annika attempted, but it was like pulling down a book and having the whole shelf toppling down on you. Elsie was on a roll, telling her exactly what she'd have done, how the worst thing she should do was play it cool.

On and on she went as Annika showered her,

though thankfully, once Annika had popped in her teeth, Elsie's train of thought drifted back to her beloved Bertie, to the sixty wonderful years they had shared, to shy kisses at the dance halls he had taken her to and the agony of him going to war. She talked about how you must never let the sun go down on a row, and she chatted away about Bertie, their wedding night and babies as Annika dressed her, combed her hair, and then wheeled her back to her room.

'You must miss him,' Annika said, arranging Elsie's table, just as she did every morning she worked there, putting her glasses within reach, her little alarm clock, and then Elsie and Bertie's wedding photo in pride of place.

'Sometimes,' Elsie said, and then her eyes were crystal-clear, 'but only when I'm sane.'

'Sorry?'

'I get to relive our moments, over and over...' Elsie smiled, and then she was gone, back to her own world, the moment of clarity over. She did not talk as Annika wrapped a shawl around her shoulders and put on her slippers.

'Enjoy it,' Annika said to her favourite resident.

He had his ticket booked, and four weeks' unpaid leave reluctantly granted. They had wanted him to take paid leave but, as Ross had pointed out, that was all saved up for his trips to Russia. This hadn't gone down too well, and Ross had sat through a thinly veiled warning from the Head of Paediatrics—there was no such thing as a part-time consultant and, while his work overseas was admirable, there were plenty of charities here in Australia he could support.

As he walked through the canteen that evening, the conversation played over in his mind. He could feel the tentacles of bureaucracy tightening around him. He wanted this day over, to be back at his farm, where there were no rules other than to make sure the animals were fed.

His intention had been to get some chocolate

from the vending machine, but he saw Annika, and thought it would be far more sensible to keep on walking. Instead, he bought a questionable cup of coffee from another machine and, uninvited, went over.

'Hi!'

He didn't ask if he could join her; he simply sat down.

She was eating a Greek salad and had pushed all the olives to one side.

'Hello.'

'Nice apron.' She was emblazoned with fairies and wands, and he could only laugh that she hated it so.

'It was the only one left,' Annika said. 'Ross, if I do write my notice—if I do give up nursing—in my letter there will be a long paragraph devoted to being made to wear aprons.'

'So you're thinking of it?'

'I don't know,' she admitted. 'I asked for a weekend off. There is a family function—there is no question that I don't go. I requested it ages ago, when I found out that I would be on the children's ward. I sent a memo, but it got lost, apparently.'

'What are you going to do?'

'Caroline has changed my late shift on Saturday to an early, and she has changed the early shift on Sunday to a late. She wasn't pleased, though, and neither am I.' She looked over to him. 'I have to get ready....' And then her voice trailed off, because it sounded ridiculous, and how could he possibly know just what getting ready for a family function entailed?

And he didn't understand her, but he wanted to.

And, yes, he was sworn off women, and she had said no to dinner, and, yes, it could get very messy, but right now he didn't care.

He should get up and go.

Yet he couldn't.

Quiet simply, he couldn't.

'I told them I'm going to Spain.'

She looked at his grim face and guessed it hadn't gone well. 'It will be worth it when you're there, I'm sure.'

'Do you ever want to go to Russia?' Ross asked. 'To see where you are from.'

'I was born here.'

'But your roots...'

'I might not like what I dig up.'

He glanced down at her plate, at the lovely ripe olives she had pushed aside. 'May I?'

'That's bad manners.'

'Not between friends.'

He would not have taken one unless she'd done what she did next and pushed the plate towards him. She watched as he took the ripe fruit and popped it in his mouth, and Annika had no idea how, but he even looked sexy as he retrieved the stone.

'They're too good to leave.'

'I don't like them,' she said. 'I tried them once...' She pulled a face.

'You were either too young to appreciate them or you got a poor effort.'

'A poor effort?'

'Olives,' Ross said, 'need to be prepared carefully. They take ages—rush them and they're bitter. I grow them at my farm, and my grand-mother knows how to make the best… She's Spanish.'

'I didn't think you were Spanish, more like a pirate or a gypsy.'

It was the first real time she had opened the conversation, the first hint at an open door. It was a glimpse that she did think about him. 'I am Spanish…' Ross said '…and I prefer Romany. I am Romany—well, my father was. My real father.'

His eyes were black—not navy, and not jade; they were as black as the leather on his belt.

'He had a brief affair with my mother when they were passing through. She was sixteen…'

'It must have caused a stir.'

'Apparently not,' Ross said. 'She was a wild thing back then—she's a bit eccentric even now. But wise…' Ross said reluctantly. 'Extremely wise.'

She wanted to know more. She didn't drain her cup or stand. She was five minutes over her coffee break, and never, ever late, yet she sat there, and then he smiled, his slow lazy smile, and she blushed. She burnt because it was bizarre, wild and crazy. She was blue-eyed and blonde and rigid, and he was so very dark and laid-back and dangerous, and they were both thinking about black-haired, blue-eyed babies, or black-eyed blonde babies, of so many fabulous combinations and the wonderful time they'd have making them.

'I have to get back.'

Annika had never flirted in her life. She had had just one boring, family-sanctioned relationship, which had ended with her rebellion in moving towards nursing, but she knew she was flirting now. She knew she was doing something dangerous and bold when she picked up a thick black olive, popped it in her mouth and then removed the pip.

'Nice?' Ross asked

'Way better than I remember.' And they weren't talking about olives, of that she was certain. She might have to check with Elsie, but she was sure she was flirting. She blushed—not from embarrassment, but because of what he said next.

'Oh, it will be.'

And as she sped back to the ward late, she was burning. She could hardly breathe as she accepted Caroline's scolding and then went to warm up a bottle for a screaming baby. Only when he was fed, changed and settled did she pull up the cot-side and let herself think.

Oh, she didn't need to run it by Elsie.

Ross had certainly been flirting.

And Annika had loved it.

CHAPTER FIVE

'I DON'T want a needle.'

Hannah was ten and scared.

She had flushed cheeks from crying, and from the virus that her body was struggling to fight, and Annika's heart went out to her, because the little girl had had enough.

Oh, she wasn't desperately ill, but she was sick and tired and wanted to be left alone. However, her IV site was due for a change, and even though cream had been applied an hour ago, so that she wouldn't feel it, she was scared and yet, Annika realised, just wanted it to be over and done with.

So too did Annika.

Ross was putting the IV in.

'I'll be in in a moment,' he had said, popping his head around the treatment room door—and

Annika had nodded and carried on chatting with Hannah, but she was exhausted from the hyper-vigilant state he put her in. She knew he was in a difficult position; he was a consultant, she a student nurse—albeit a mature one. She also knew a relationship was absolutely the last thing she needed. Chaos abounded in her life; there was just so much to sort out.

Yet she wanted him.

Elsie, when Annika had discussed it with her, had huffed and puffed that it should be Ross who asked *her* out, Ross who should take her out dancing. But things were different now, Annika had pointed out, and she'd already said no to him once.

'Ask him,' Cecil had said when she had taken him in his evening drink. He had a nip of brandy each night, and always asked for another one. 'You lot say you want equal rights, but only when it suits you. Why should he risk his job?'

'Risk his job?'

'For harassing you?' Cecil said stoutly. 'He's

already asked you and you said no—if you've changed your mind, then bloody well ask him. Stop playing games.'

'How do you know all this?' Annika had demanded, and then gone straight to Elsie's room. 'That was a secret.'

'I've got dementia.' Elsie huffed. 'You can't expect me to keep a secret.'

'You cunning witch!' Annika said, and Elsie laughed.

She hadn't just told Cecil either!

Half of the residents were asking for updates, and then sulking when Annika reported that there were none.

So, when Ross had asked her to bring Hannah up to the treatment room to have her IV bung replaced, even though Cassie had offered to do it for her, Annika had bitten the bullet. Now she was trying to talk to her patient.

'The cream we have put on your arm means that you won't feel it.'

'I just don't like it.'

'I know,' Annika said, 'but once it is done you

can go back to bed and have a nice rest and you won't be worrying about it any more. Dr Ross is very gentle.'

'I am.'

She hadn't heard him come in, and she gave him a small smile as she turned around to greet him.

'Hannah's nervous.'

'I bet you are,' Ross said to his patient. 'You had a tough time of it in Emergency, didn't you? Hannah was too sick to wait for the anaesthetic cream to work,' he explained to Annika, but really for the little girl's benefit, 'and she was also so ill that her veins were hard to find, so the doctor had to have a few goes.'

'It hurt,' Hannah gulped.

'I know it did.' Ross was checking the trolley and making sure everything was set up before he commenced. Hannah was lying down, but she looked as if at any moment she might jump off the treatment bed. 'But the doctor in Emergency wasn't a children's doctor...' Ross winked to Hannah, 'I'm used to little veins, and you're not as sick now, so they're going to be a lot easier to find and because of the cream you won't be able to feel it...'

'No!'

She was starting to really cry now, pulling her arm away as Ross slipped on a tourniquet. The panic that had been building was coming to the fore. He did his best to calm her, but she wasn't having it. She needed this IV; she had already missed her six a.m. medication, and she was vomiting and not able to hold down any fluids.

'Hannah, you need this,' Ross said, and as she had done for several patients now, Annika leant over her, keeping her little body as still as she could as Ross tried to reassure her.

'Don't look,' Annika said, holding the little girl's frightened gaze. 'You won't feel anything.'

'Just because I can't see it, I still know that you're hurting me!' came the pained little voice, and something inside Annika twisted. She felt so hopeless; she truly didn't know what to say, or how to comfort the girl.

'Watch, then,' Ross said. 'Let her go.'

He smiled to Annika and she did so, sure that the little girl would jump down from the treatment bed and run, but instead she lay there, staring suspiciously up at Ross.

'I know you've been hurt,' he said, 'and I know that in Emergency it would have been painful because the doctor had to have a few goes to get the needle in, but I'm not going to hurt you.'

'What if you can't get the needle in, like last time?'

'I'm quite sure I can,' Ross said, pressing on a rather nice vein with his olive-skinned finger. 'But if, for whatever reason, I can't, then we'll put some cream elsewhere—you're not as sick now, and we can wait…'

His voice was completely serious; he wasn't doing the smiling, reassuring thing that Annika rather poorly attempted.

'I am going to do everything I can not to hurt you. If for some reason there's ever a procedure that will hurt, I will tell you, and we'll work it out, but this one,' Ross said, 'isn't going to hurt.'

He tightened the tourniquet and Hannah

watched. He swabbed the vein a couple of times and then got out the needle, and she didn't cry or move away, she just watched.

'Even I'm nervous now.' Ross grinned, and so too did Annika, that tiny pause lifting the mood in the room. Even Hannah managed a little smile. She stared as the needle went in, and flinched, but only because she was expecting pain. When it didn't come, when the needle was in and Ross was taping it securely in place, her grin grew much wider when Ross told her she had been very brave.

'Very brave!' Annika said, like a parrot, because she could never be as at ease with children as he was. She was attaching the IV and Ross was looking through his drug book, working out the new medication regime that he wanted Hannah on.

Brighter now it was all over, Hannah looked up at Annika.

'You're pretty.'

'Thank you.' She hated this. It was okay when Elsie said it, or one of the oldies, but children

were so probing. Annika was still trying to attach
the bung, but the little hard bit of plastic proved
fiddly, and the last thing she wanted was to mess
up the IV access. She almost did when Hannah
spoke next.

'Have you got a boyfriend?'

'No.' Her cheeks were on fire, and she could
feel Ross looking at her, though she was *so* not
going to look at him.

'I thought you did, Annika.' He spoke then to
Hannah. 'He's a very nice guy, apparently.'

'It's very early days.' The drip was attached,
and now she had to strap it in place.

'I like a boy in my class,' Hannah said, with
a confidence Annika would never possess. 'He
sent me a card, and he wrote that he's coming
to visit me once I'm allowed visitors that aren't
my mum.'

'That's nice.'

'So, where does your boyfriend take you?'
Hannah probed.

'I'm more a stay-at-home person…' Annika
blew at her fringe and pressed in the numbers.

Ross was beside her, checking that the dosage was correct and signing off on the sheet. She could feel that he was laughing, knew he was enjoying her discomfort—and there and then she decided to be brave.

Exceptionally brave—and if it didn't work she'd blame Cecil and Elsie.

'I was thinking of asking him over for dinner on Saturday.' Annika swallowed. She knew her face was on fire, she was cringing and burning, and yet she was also excited.

'That sounds nice. I'm sure he'd love it,' was all Ross said.

She got Hannah back to bed, and then, as she went back into the treatment room to prepare Luke's dressing, Ross came in.

'I don't want to talk at work.'

'Fine.'

'So can we just keep things separate?'

'No problem, Annika.'

'I mean it, Ross.'

'Of course,' he said patiently. 'Annika, do you

know where the ten gauge needles are kept? They've run out on the IV trolley...'

And he was so matter-of-fact, so absolutely normal in his behaviour towards her, that Annika wondered if she actually had asked him out at all. At six a.m. on a Saturday, when he hadn't asked for a time, or even an address, she wasn't sure that she had.

CHAPTER SIX

'How's the children's ward?' Elsie was wide awake before Annika had even flicked the lights on.

'It's okay,' Annika said, and then she admitted the truth. 'I'll be glad when it's over.'

'What have you got next?'

'Maternity,' Annika said, as Elsie slurped her tea.

She seemed to have caught her second wind these past few days: more and more she was lucid, and the lucid times were lasting longer too. She was getting over that nasty UTI, Dianne, the Div 1 nurse had explained. They often caused confusion in the elderly, or, as in Elsie's case, exacerbated dementia. It was good to have her back.

'I'm not looking forward to it.'

'What *are* you looking forward to?'

'I don't know,' Annika admitted.

'How's your boyfriend?' Elsie asked when they were in the shower, Annika in her gumboots, Elsie in her little shower chair. 'How's Ross?'

'I don't know that either,' Annika said, cringing a little when Elsie said his name. 'It's complicated.'

'Love isn't complicated,' Elsie said. 'You are.'

And they had a laugh, a real laugh, as she dried and dressed Elsie and put her in her chair. Then Annika did something she had never done before.

'I've got something for you.' Nervous, she went to the fridge and brought out her creation.

It was a white chocolate box, filled with chocolate mousse and stuffed with raspberries.

'Where's my toast?' Elsie asked, and that made Annika laugh. Then the old lady peered at the creation and dipped her bony finger into the mousse, licked it, and had a raspberry. 'You bought this for me?'

'I made it,' Annika said. 'This was my practice one…' She immediately apologised. 'Sorry, that sounds rude…'

'It doesn't sound rude at all.'

'You have to spread the white chocolate on parchment paper and then slice it; you only fill the boxes at the end. I did a course a few years ago,' Annika admitted. 'Well, I didn't finish it…'

'You didn't need to,' Elsie said. 'You could serve this up every night and he'd be happy. This is all you need…it's delicious…' Elsie was cramming raspberries in her mouth. 'This is for your man?'

'I'm worried he'll think I've gone to too much effort.'

'Is he worth the effort?' Elsie asked.

'Yes.'

'Then don't worry.'

'I think I've asked him to dinner tonight.'

'You think?' Elsie frowned. 'What did he say?'

'That it sounded very nice.' Annika gulped.

'Only we haven't confirmed times. I'm not even sure he knows where I live...'

'He can find out,' Elsie said.

'How?'

'If he wants to, he will.'

'So I shouldn't ring him and check...?'

'Oh, no!' Elsie said. 'Absolutely not.'

'What if he doesn't come?'

'You have to trust that he will.'

'But what if he doesn't?'

'Then you bring in the food for us lot tomorrow,' Elsie said. 'Of course he's coming.' She put her hands on Annika's cheeks. 'Of *course* he'll come.'

CHAPTER SEVEN

IT KILLED her not to ring or page him, but Elsie had been adamant.

She had to trust that he would come, and if he didn't… Well, he had never been going to.

So, when she finished at the nursing home at nine a.m., she went home and had a little sleep, and then went to the Victoria Market. She bought some veal, some cream, the most gorgeous mushrooms, some fresh fettuccini and, of course, some more raspberries.

It was nice to be in the kitchen and stretching herself again.

Melting chocolate, whisking in eggs—she really had loved cooking and learning, but cooking at a high level had to be a passion. It was an absolute passion that Annika had realised she didn't have.

But still, she could love it.

She didn't know what to wear. She'd gone to so much trouble with the dessert that she didn't want to make too massive an effort with her clothes, in case she terrified him.

She opened her wardrobe and stared at a couple of Kolovsky creations. She had a little giggle to herself, wondering about his reaction if she opened the door to him in red velvet, but settled for a white skirt and a lilac top. She put on some lilac sandals, but she never wore shoes at home—well, not at this home—and ten minutes in she had kicked them off. She was dusting the chocolate boxes and trying not to care that it was ten past eight. She checked her hair, which was for once out of its ponytail, and put on some lip-gloss. Then she went to the kitchen, opened the fridge. The chocolate boxes hadn't collapsed, and the veal was all sliced and floured and waiting—and then she heard the knock at her door.

'Hi.' His voice made her stomach shrink.

'Hi.'

He was holding flowers, and she was so glad that she had taken Elsie's advice and not rung.

He kissed her on the cheek and handed her the flowers—glorious flowers, all different, wild and fragrant, and tied together with a bow. 'Hand-picked,' he said, 'which is why I'm so late.'

And she smiled, because of course they weren't. He'd been to some trendy place, no doubt, but she was grateful for them, because they got her through those first awkward moments as he followed her into the kitchen and she located a vase and filled it with water.

Ross was more than a little perplexed.

He hadn't known quite what to expect from tonight, but he hadn't expected this.

Okay, he'd known from her address that she wasn't in the smartest suburb. He hadn't given it that much thought till he'd entered her street. A trendy converted townhouse, perhaps, he'd thought as he'd pulled up—a Kolovsky attempt at pretending to be poor.

Except her car stuck out like a sore thumb in the street, and as he climbed the steps he saw there was nothing trendy or converted about her flat.

There was an ugly floral carpet, cheap blinds dressed the windows, and not a single thing matched.

The kitchen was a mixture of beige and brown and a little bit of taupe too!

There was a party going on upstairs, and an argument to the left and right. Here in the centre was Annika.

She didn't belong—so much so he wanted to grab her by the hand and take her back to the farm right now, right this minute.

'I'll start dinner.'

She poured some oil in a large wok, turned the gas up on some simmering water, and then glanced over and gave him a nervous smile, which he returned. Then she slipped on an apron.

And it transformed her.

He stood and watched as somehow the tiny kitchen changed.

She pulled open the fridge and put a little meat

in the wok. It was rather slow to sizzle, so she pulled out of the fridge some prepared plates, and he watched as she tipped coils of fresh pasta into the water and then threw the rest of the meat into the wok. Her hair was in the way, so she tied it back in a knot. He just carried on watching as this awkward, difficult woman relaxed and transformed garlic, pepper, cream and wine. He had never thought watching someone cook could be so sexy, yet before the water had even returned to the boil Ross was standing on the other side of the bench!

'Okay?' Annika checked.

'Great,' Ross said.

In seven minutes they were at the table—all those dishes, in a matter of moments, blended into a veal scaloppini that was to die for.

'When you said dinner...'

'I love to cook...'

And she loved to eat too.

With food between them, and with wine, somehow, gradually, it got easier.

He told her about his farm—that his sisters

didn't get it, but it must be the gypsy blood in him because there he felt he belonged.

'I've never been to a farm.'

'Never?'

'No.'

'You're a city girl?'

'I guess,' Annika said.

She intrigued him.

'You used to model?'

'For a couple of years,' Annika said. 'Only in-house.'

'Sorry?'

'Just for Kolovsky,' she explained. 'I always thought that was what I wanted to do—well, it was expected of me, really—but when I got there it was just hours and hours in make-up, hours and hours hanging around, and...' she rolled her eyes '...no dinners like this.' She registered his frown. 'Thin wasn't thin enough, and I like my food too much.'

'So you went to Paris...?'

'I did.'

'What made you decide to do nursing?'

'I'm not sure,' Annika admitted. 'When my father was ill I watched the nurses caring for him...' It was hard to explain, so she didn't. 'What about you? Are you the same as Iosef? Is medicine your vocation?'

'Being a doctor was the only thing I ever wanted to be.'

'Lucky you.'

'Though when I go to Russia with your brother, sometimes I wonder if there is more than being a doctor in a well-equipped city hospital.'

'You're not happy at work?'

'I'm very happy at work,' Ross corrected. 'Sometimes, though, I feel hemmed in—often I feel hemmed in. I just broke up with someone because of it.' He gave her a wry smile. 'I'm supposed to be sworn off women.'

'I'm not good at hemming.'

Ross laughed. 'I can't picture you with a needle.' And then he was serious. 'Romanys have this image of being cads—that is certainly my mother's take. I understand that, but really they are loyal to commitment, and virginity is important to them, which is why they often marry young...' He gave an embarrassed half-laugh. 'There is more to them than I understand...'

'And you need to find out?'

'I think so,' Ross answered. 'Maybe that is why I get on with the orphans in Russia. I am much luckier, of course, but I can relate to them—to that not knowing, never fully knowing where you came from. I don't know my father's history.'

'You could have a touch of Russian in you!' Annika smiled.

'Who knows?' Ross smiled. 'Do you go back to Russia?'

She shook her head. 'Levander does, Iosef as you know does work there...'

'Aleksi?' Ross asked.

'He goes, but not for work...' She gave a shrug. 'I don't really know why. I've just never felt the need to.'

'You speak Russian, though?'

'No.' She shook her head. 'Only a little—a very little compared to my family.'

'You have an accent.'

'Because I refused to speak Russian…' She smiled at his bemusement. 'I was a very wilful child. I spoke Russian and a little English till I was five, and then I realised that we lived in Australia. I started to say I didn't understand Russian—that I only understood English, wanted to speak English.' He smiled at the image of her as a stubborn five-year-old. 'It infuriated my mother, and my teacher… I learnt English from Russians, which is why I have an accent. Do you speak Spanish?'

'Not as much as I'd like to.'

'You're going in a couple of weeks?'

'Yeah.' And he told her—well, bits… 'Mum's upset about it. I think she's worried I'm going to find my real father and set up camp with him. Run away and leave it all behind…'

'Are you?'

'No.' Ross shook his head. 'I'd like to meet him, get to know him if I can find him. I only have his first name.'

'Which is?'

'Reyes,' Ross said, and then he gave her a little

part of him that he didn't usually share. 'That's actually my real name.'

'I lived with my father. Every day I saw him,' Annika said, giving back a little part of herself, 'but I don't think I knew him at all.'

'I know about Levander.' He watched her swallow. 'I know that Levander was raised in the Detsky Dom.'

'Iosef shouldn't talk.'

'Iosef and I have spent weeks—no, months, working in Russian orphanages. It's tough going there—sometimes you need to talk. He hates that Levander was raised there.'

'My parents were devastated when they found out…' She was glad she'd read that press release now. 'On his deathbed my father begged that we set up the foundation…' Her voice cracked. She was caught between the truth and a lie, and she didn't know what was real any more. 'We are holding a big fundraiser soon. If nursing doesn't work out then I am thinking of working full-time on the board…'

'Organising fundraisers?'

'Perhaps.' She shrugged. 'I'll get dessert…'

'You made these?' He couldn't believe it. He took a bite and couldn't believe it again—and then he said the completely wrong thing. 'You're wasted as a nurse.'

And he saw her eyes shutter.

'I'm sorry, Annika; I didn't mean it like that.'

'Don't worry.' She smiled. 'You're probably right.'

'Not wasted…'

'Just leave it.'

'I can't leave it,' Ross said, and her eyes jerked up to his. 'But I ought to.'

'At least till I have finished on the ward,' Annika said, and her throat was so tight she didn't know how to swallow, and her chocolate box sat unopened.

'I'll be in Spain,' Ross said.

'Slow is good.' Annika nodded. 'I don't want to rush.'

'So we just put it on hold?' Ross checked, and she nodded. 'Just have dinner?' He winced. 'When I say *just*…'

'Maybe one kiss goodnight,' Annika relented, because Elsie would be so disappointed other-wise.

'Sounds good,' Ross said. 'Now or later?'

'You choose.'

Four hours of preparation: tempering the chocolate, slicing the boxes, choosing the best raspberries. And the mousse recipe was a complicated one. All that work, all those hours, slipped deliciously away as he pulled her across the table and her breast sank into her own creation.

His tongue tasted better than anything she could conjure. They both had to stretch, but it was worth it. He tasted of chocolate, and then of him. His hair was in her fingers and she was pressing her face into him, the scratch of his jaw, the press of his lips. She wanted more, so badly she almost climbed onto the table just to be closer, but it was easier to stand. Lips locked, they kissed over the table, and then did a sort of crab walk till they could properly touch—and touch they did.

The most touching it was possible to do with clothes on and standing. She felt his lovely bum, and his jeans, and she pressed him into her. It was still just a kiss, one kiss, but it went on for ever.

'Oh, Annika,' he said, when she pulled back for a gulp of air, and then he saw the mess on her top and set to work.

'That's not kissing…' He was kissing her breast through the fabric, sucking off the mousse and the cream, and her fingers were back in his hair.

'It is,' he said.

And the raspberries had made the most terrible stain, so he concentrated on getting it out, and then she had to stop him. She stepped back and did something she never did.

She started to laugh.

And then she did something really stupid—something she'd cringe at when she told Elsie—well, the edited version—but knew Elsie would clap her approval.

She told him to dance—ordered him, in fact!

She lay on the sofa and watched, and there was rather more noise than usual from Annika's flat—not that the neighbours noticed.

She lay there and watched as his great big black boots stamped across the floor, and it was mad, really, but fantastic. She could smell the gypsy bonfire, and she knew he could too—it was their own fantasy, crazy and sort of private, but she would tell Elsie just a little.

And she did only kiss him—maybe once or twice, or three times more.

But who knew the places you could go to with a kiss?

Who knew you could be standing pressed against the door fully dressed, but naked in your mind?

'Bad girl,' Ross said as, still standing, she landed back on earth.

'Oh, I will be!' Annika said.

'Come back to the farm...'

'We said slowly.'

So they had—and there was Spain, and according to form he knew he'd hurt her, but he was suddenly sure that he wouldn't. She could take a sledgehammer to his bedroom wall if she chose, and he'd just lie on the bed and let her.

'Come to the farm.' God, what was he doing?

'I've got stuff too, Ross.'

'I know, I know.'

'Don't rush me.'

'I know.' He was coming back to earth as well. He'd never been accused of rushing things before. It was always Ross pulling back, always Ross reluctant to share—it felt strange to be on the other side.

'And I've never been bad.'

He started to laugh, and then he realised she wasn't joking.

'The rules are different if you're a Kolovsky girl, and till recently I've never been game enough to break them.'

Oh!

Looking into her troubled eyes, knowing what he knew about her family, suddenly he was scared of his own reputation and knew it was time to back off.

Annika Kolovsky he couldn't risk hurting.

CHAPTER EIGHT

AT HER request, things slowed down.

Stopped, really.

The occasional text, a lot of smiles, and a couple of coffees in the canteen.

It was just as well, really. There was no time for a relationship as her world rapidly unravelled.

Aleksi had hit a journalist and was on the front pages again.

Her mother was in full charity ball mode, and nothing Annika could say or do at work was right.

'He's *that* sick from chicken pox?' Annika couldn't help but speak up during handover. Normally she kept her head down and just wrote, but it was so appalling she couldn't help it. An eight-year-old had been admitted from Emergency with encephalitis and was semiconscious—all from a simple virus. 'You can get *that* ill from chicken pox?'

'It's unusual,' Caroline said, 'but, yes. If he doesn't improve then he'll be transferred to the children's hospital. For now he's on antiviral medication and hourly obs. His mother is, of course, beside herself. She's got two others at home who have the virus too. Ross is just checking with Infectious Diseases and then he'll be contacting their GP to prescribe antivirals for them too.' Caroline was so matter-of-fact, and Annika knew she had to be too, but she found it so hard!

Gowning up, wearing a mask, dealing with the mum.

She checked the IV solutions with a nurse and punched in the numbers on the IVAC that would deliver the correct dosage of the vital medication. She tried to wash the child as gently as she could when the Div 1 nurse left. The room was impossibly hot, especially when she was all gowned up, but any further infection for him would be disastrous.

'Thank you so much.' The poor, petrified mum took time to thank Annika as she gently rolled the boy and changed the sheets. 'How do you think he's doing?'

Annika felt like a fraud.

She stood caught in the headlamps of the mother's anxious gaze. How could she tell her that she had no idea, that till an hour ago she hadn't realised chicken pox could make anyone so ill and that she was petrified for the child too?

'His observations are stable,' Annika said carefully.

'But how do *you* think he's doing?' the mother pushed, and Annika didn't know what to say. 'Is there something that you're not telling me?'

The mother was getting more and more upset, and so Annika said what she had been told to in situations such as this.

'I'll ask the nurse in charge to speak with you.'

* * *

It was her first proper telling-off on the children's Ward.

Well, it wasn't a telling-off but a pep talk—and rather a long one—because it wasn't an isolated incident, apparently.

Heather Jameson came down, and she sat as Caroline tried to explain the error of Annika's ways.

'Ross is in there now.' Caroline let out a breath. 'The mother thought from Annika's reaction that there was bad news on the way.'

'She asked me how I thought he was doing,' Annika said. 'I hadn't seen him before. I had nothing to compare it with. So I said I would get the nurse in charge to speak with her.'

She hadn't done anything wrong—but it was just another example of how she couldn't get it right.

It was the small talk, the chats, the comfort she was so bad at.

'Mum's fine.' Ross knocked and walked in. 'She's exhausted. Her son's ill. She's just searching for clues, Annika.' He looked over to her. 'You didn't do anything wrong. In fact he is improving—but you couldn't have known that.'

So it was good news—only for Annika it didn't feel like it.

'It's not a big deal,' Ross said later, catching her in the milk room, where she was trying to sort out bottles for the late shift.

'It is to me,' Annika said, hating her own awkwardness. She should be pleased that her shift was over, and tonight she didn't have to work at the nursing home, but tonight she was going to her mother's for dinner.

'Why don't we—?'

'You're not helping, Ross,' Annika said. 'Can you just be a doctor at work, please?'

'Sure.'

And she wanted to call him back—to say sorry for biting his head off—but it was dinner at her mother's, and no one could ever understand what a nightmare that was.

* * *

'How's the children's ward?'

Iosef and Annie were there too, which would normally have made things easier—but not tonight. They had avoided the subject of Aleksi's latest scandal. They had spoken a little about the ball, and then they'd begun to eat in silence.

'It's okay,' Annika said, pushing her food around her plate.

'But not great?' Iosef checked.

'No.'

They'd been having the same conversation for months now.

She'd started off in nursing so enthusiastically, raving about her placements, about the different patients, but gradually, just as Iosef had predicted, the gloss had worn off.

As it had in modelling.

And cooking

And in jewellery design.

'How's Ross?' Iosef asked, and luckily he missed her blush because Nina made a snorting sound.

'Filthy gypsy.'

'You've always been *so* welcoming to my friends!' Iosef retorted. 'He does a lot of good work for your chosen charity.' There was a muscle pounding in Iosef's cheek and they still hadn't got through the main course.

'Romany!' Annika said, gesturing to one of the staff to fill up her wine. 'He prefers the word Romany to gypsy.'

'And I prefer not to speak of it while I eat my dinner,' Nina said, then fixed Annika with a stare. 'No more wine.'

'It's my second glass.'

'And you have the ball soon—you'll be lucky to get into your dress as it is.'

There was that feeling again. For months now out of nowhere it would bubble up, and she would suddenly feel like crying—but she never, ever did.

What she did do instead, and her hand was shaking as she did it, was take another sip of wine, and for the first time in memory in front of her mother she finished everything on her plate.

'How are you finding the work?' Iosef attempted again as Nina glared at her daughter.

'It's a lot harder than I thought it would be.'

'I was the same in my training,' Annie said happily, sitting back a touch as seconds were ladled onto her plate.

Annika wanted seconds too, but she knew better than to push it. The air was so toxic she felt as if she were choking on it, and then she stared at her brother, and for the first time ever she thought she saw a glimmer of sympathy there.

Annie chatted on. 'I thought about leaving—nursing wasn't at all what I'd imagined—then I did my Emergency placement and I realised I'd found my niche.'

'I just don't know if it's for me,' Annika said.

'Of course it isn't for you,' Nina said. 'You're a Kolovsky.'

'Is there anything you want help with?' Iosef offered, ignoring his mother's unhelpful comment. 'Annie or I can go over things with you. We can go through your assignments…'

He was trying, Annika knew that, and because he was her brother she loved him—it was just that they had never got on.

They were chalk and cheese. Iosef, like his twin Aleksi, was as dark as she was blonde. They were both driven, both relentless in their different pursuits, whereas all her life Annika had drifted.

They had teased her, of course, as brothers always did. She'd been the apple of her parents' eyes, had just had to shed a tear or pout and whatever she wanted was hers. She had adored her parents, and simply hadn't been able to understand the arguments after Levander, her stepbrother, had arrived.

Till then her life had seemed perfect.

Levander had come from Russia, an angry, displaced teenager. His past was shocking, but her father had done his best to make amends for the son he hadn't known about all those years. Ivan had brought him into the family and given him everything.

Annika truly hadn't understood the rows, the

hate, the anger that had simmered beneath the surface of her family. She had ached for peace, for the world to go back to how it was before.

But, worse than that, she had started to wonder why the charmed life she led made her so miserable.

She had been sucked so deep into the centre of the perfect world that had been created for her it had been almost impossible to climb out and search for answers. She couldn't even fathom the questions.

Yet she *was* trying.

'You could do much better for the poor orphans if you worked on the foundation's board,' Nina said. 'Have you thought about it?'

'A bit,' Annika admitted.

'You could be an ambassador for the Kolovskys. It is good for the company to show we take our charity work seriously.'

'And very good for you if it ever gets out that Ivan's firstborn was a Detsky Dom boy.' Iosef had had enough; he stood from his seat.

'Iosef!' Nina reprimanded him—but Iosef was

still, after all these years, furious at what had happened to his brother. He had worked in the orphanages himself and was struggling to forgive the fact that Levander had been raised there.

'I'm going home.'

'You haven't had dessert.'

'Annie is on an early shift in the morning.'

Annie gathered up the baby, and Annika kissed her little niece and tried to make small talk with Annie as Iosef said goodbye to her mother, who remained seated.

'Can I hold her?' Annika asked, and she did. It felt so different from holding one of the babies at work. She stared into grey trusting eyes that were like the baby's father's, and smiled at the knot of dark curls that came from her mother. She smelt as sweet as a baby should. Annika buried her face in her niece's and blew a kiss on her cheek till she giggled.

'Annika?' Iosef gestured her out to the hall. 'Would some money help?'

'I don't want your money.'

'You're having to support yourself,' Iosef

pointed out. 'Hell, I know what she can be like—I had to put myself through medical school.'

'But you did it.'

'And it was hard,' Iosef said. 'And…' He let out a breath. 'I was never their favourite.' He didn't mean it as an insult; he was speaking the truth. Iosef had always been strong, had always done his own thing. Annika was only now finding out that she could. 'How *are* you supporting yourself?'

'I'm doing some shifts in a nursing home.'

'Oh, Annika!' It was Annie who stepped in. 'You must be exhausted.'

'It's not bad. I actually like it.'

'Look…' Iosef wrote out a cheque, but Annika shook her head. 'Just concentrate on the nursing. Then—*then*,' he reiterated, 'you can find out if you actually like it.'

She could…

'Give your studies a proper chance,' Iosef said.

She stared at the cheque, which covered a year's wage in the nursing home. Maybe this way she *could* concentrate just on nursing. But it hurt to swallow her pride.

'We've got to go.'

And they did. They opened the front door and Annika stood there. She stroked Rebecca's cheek and it dawned on her that not once had Nina held or even looked at the baby.

Her own grandchild, her own blood, was leaving, and because she loathed the mother Nina hadn't even bothered to stand. She could so easily turn her back.

So what would she be like to a child that wasn't her own?

'Iosef...' She followed him out to the car. Annie was putting Rebecca in the baby seat and even though it was warm Annika was shivering. 'Did they know?'

'What are you talking about, Annika?'

'Levander?' Annika gulped. 'Did they know he was in the orphanage?'

'Just leave it.'

'I can't leave it!' Annika begged. 'You're so full of hate, Levander too...but in everything else you're reasonable. Levander would have forgiven them for not knowing. You would too.'

He didn't answer.

She wanted to hit him for not answering, for not denying it, for not slapping her and telling her she was wrong.

'You should have told me.'

'Why?' Iosef asked. 'So you can have the pleasure of hating them too?'

'Come home with us,' Annie said, putting her arm around Annika. 'Come back with us and we can talk...'

'I don't want to.'

'Come on, Annika,' Iosef said. 'I'll tell Mum you're not feeling well.'

'I can't,' Annika said. 'I can't just leave...'

'Yes, Annika,' Iosef said, 'you can—you can walk away this minute if you want to!'

'You still come here!' Annika pointed out. 'Mum ignores every word Annie ever says but you still come for dinner, still sit there...'

'For you,' Iosef said, and that halted her. 'The way she is with Annie, with my daughter, about my friends… Do you really think I want to be here? Annie and I are here for you.'

Annika didn't fully believe it, and she couldn't walk away either. She didn't want to hate her mother, didn't want the memory of her father to change, so instead she ate a diet jelly and fruit dessert with Nina, who started crying when it was time for Annika to go home.

'Always Iosef blames me. I hardly see Aleksi unless I go into the office, and now you have left home.'

'I'm twenty-five.'

'And you would rather have no money and do a job you hate than work in the family business, where you belong,' Nina said, and Annika closed her eyes in exhaustion. 'I understand that maybe you want your own home, but at least if you worked for the family… Annika, think about it—think of the good you could do! You are not even *liking* nursing. The charity ball next week will raise hundreds of thousands of dollars— surely you are better overseeing that, and making it bigger each year, than working in a job you don't like?'

'You knew about Levander, didn't you?' Had Annika thought about it, she'd never have had the courage to ask, but she didn't think, she just said it—and then she added something else. 'If you hit me again you'll never see me again, so I suggest that you talk to me instead.'

'I was pregnant with twins,' Nina hissed. 'It was hard enough to flee Russia just us two—we would never have got out with him.'

'So you left him?'

'To save my sons!' Nina said. 'Yes.'

'How could Pa?' Still she couldn't cry, but it was there at the back of her throat. 'How could he leave him behind?'

'He didn't know...' Annika had seen her mother cry, had heard her wail, but she had never seen her crumple. 'For years I did not tell him. He thought his son was safe with his mother. Only I knew...'

'Knew what?'

'We were ready to leave, and that *blyat* comes to

the door with her bastard son…' Annika winced at her mother's foul tongue, and yet unlike her brothers she listened, heard that Levander's mother had turned up one night with a small toddler and pleaded that Nina take him, that she was dying, that her family were too poor to keep the little boy…

'I was pregnant, Annika…' Nina sobbed. 'I was big, the doctor said there were two, I wanted my babies to have a chance. We would never have got out with Levander.'

'You could have tried.'

'And if we'd failed?' Nina pleaded. 'Then what?' she demanded. 'So I sent Levander and his mother away, and for years your father never found out.'

'And when he did Levander came here?'

'No.' Nina was finally honest. 'We tried for a few more years to pretend all was perfect.' She looked over to her daughter. 'So now you can hate me too.'

CHAPTER NINE

BUT Annika didn't want to hate her mother.

She just didn't know how to love her right now.

She wanted Ross.

She wanted to hide in his arms and fall asleep.

She wanted to go over and over it with him.

The truth was so much worse than the lies, and yet she could sort of understand her mother's side.

The family secret had darkened many shades, and her mother had begged her not to tell anyone.

Oh, Annie knew, and no doubt so did Millie, Levander's wife, but they were real partners. Ross and Annika...they were brand spanking new!

How could she land it on him?

And anyway, he would soon be heading off for Spain!

For the first time in her life she had a tangible reason to sever ties with her mother. Instead she found herself there more and more, listening to Nina's stories, understanding a little more what had driven her parents, what had fuelled their need for the castle they had built for their children.

'I haven't seen you so much,' Elsie commented.

'I've cut down my shifts,' Annika said, with none of her old sparkle. 'I need to concentrate on my studies.'

Cashing the cheque had hurt, but then so too did everything right now. When push had come to shove, she'd realised that she actually *liked* her shifts at the nursing home, so instead of cutting ties completely, she'd drastically reduced her hours.

Ross was around, and though they smiled and said hello she kept him at a distance.

She had spent the past week in cots, which didn't help matters.

The babies were so tiny and precious, and sometimes so ill it terrified Annika.

She was constantly checking that she had put the cot-sides up, and double- and triple-checking medicine doses.

She longed to be like the other nurses, who bounced a babe on their knee and fed with one hand while juggling the phone with the other.

She just couldn't.

'How's that man of yours?' Elsie asked, because Annika was unusually quiet.

'He goes to Spain soon—when he gets back we will maybe see each other some more.'

'Why wait?'

'You know he's a doctor—a senior doctor on my ward?'

'Oh.' Elsie pondered. 'I'm sure others have managed—you can be discreet.'

'There's stuff going on.' Annika combed through her hair. 'With my family. I think it's a bit soon to land it all on him.'

'If he's the right one for you, he'll be able to take it,' Elsie said.

'Ah, but if he's not…' Annika could almost see the news headlines. 'How do you know if you can trust someone?'

'You don't know,' Elsie said. 'You never know. You just hope.'

CHAPTER TEN

Ross always liked to get to work early.

He liked a quick chat with the night staff, if possible, to hear from them how things were going on the ward, rather than hear the second-hand version a few hours later from the day nurses.

It was a routine that worked for him well.

A niggle from a night nurse could become a full-blown incident by ten a.m. For Ross it was easier to buy a coffee and the paper, have a quick check with the night staff and then have ten minutes to himself before the day began in earnest. This morning there was no such luxury. He'd been at work all night, and at six-thirty had just made his way from ICU when he stopped by the nurses' station.

'Luke's refused to have his blood sugar taken,'

Amy, the night nurse, explained. 'I was just talking him round to it and his mum arrived.'

'Great!' Ross rolled his eyes. 'Don't tell me she took it herself?'

'Yep.'

It had been said so many times, but sometimes working on a children's ward would be so much easier without the parents!

'Okay—I'll have another word. What else?'

There wasn't much—it was busy but under control—and so Ross escaped to his office, took a sip of the best coffee in Australia and opened the paper. He stared and he read and he stared, and if *his* morning wasn't going too well, then someone else's wasn't, either.

His pager went off, and he saw that it was a call from Iosef Kolovsky. He took it.

'Hi.'

'Sorry to call you for private business.' Iosef was, as always, straight to the point. 'Have you seen the paper?'

'Just.'

'Okay—now, I think Annika is on your ward

at the moment…' Iosef had never asked for a favour in his life. 'Could you just keep an eye out for her—and if the staff are talking tell them that what has been written is nonsense? You have my permission to say you know me well and that this is all rubbish.'

'Will do,' Ross said, and, because he knew he would get no more from Iosef, 'How's Annie?'

'Swearing at the newspaper.'

'I bet. I'll do what I can.'

He rang off and read it again. It was a scathing piece—mainly about Iosef's twin Aleksi.

On his father's death two years ago he had taken over as chief of the House of Kolovsky, and now, the reporter surmised, Ivan Kolovsky the founder must be turning in his grave.

There had been numerous staff cuts, but Aleksi, it was said, was frittering away the family fortune in casinos, on long exotic trips, and on indiscretions with women. A bitter ex, who was allegedly nine weeks pregnant by him, was savage in her observations. Not only had staff been cut, but his own sister, a talented jewellery designer, had been cut off from the family trust and was now living in a small one-bedroom flat, studying nursing. Along with a few pictures of Aleksi looking rather the worse for wear were two of Annika—one of her in a glamorous ballgown, looking sleek and groomed, and the other... Well, it must have been a bad day, because she was in her uniform and looking completely exhausted, teary even, as she stepped out into the ambulance bay.

There was even a quote from an anonymous source that stated how miserable she was in her job, how she hated every moment, and how she thought she was better than that.

How, Ross had fathomed, was she supposed to walk into work after that?

She did, though.

He was sitting in the staffroom when she entered, just as the morning TV news show chatted about the piece. An orthopaedic surgeon was reading the paper, and a couple of colleagues were discussing it as she walked in. Ross felt his heart squeeze in mortification for her.

But she didn't look particularly tense, and she didn't look flushed or teary—for a moment he was worried that she didn't even know what was being said.

Until she sat down, eating her raisin toast from the canteen, and a colleague jumped up to turn the television over.

'It's fine,' she said. 'I've already seen it.'

The only person, Ross surmised as the gathering staff sat there, who didn't seem uncomfortable was Annika.

Ross called her back as the day staff left for handover. 'How are you doing?'

'Fine.'

'If you want to talk…?'

'Then I'll speak with my family.'

Ross's lips tightened. She didn't make things easy, but he didn't have the luxury of thinking up a smart retort as his pager had summoned him to a meeting.

'I'm here if you need me, okay?'

* * *

The thing with children, Annika was fast realising, was that they weren't dissimilar from the residents in the nursing home. There, the residents' tact buttons had long since been switched off—on the children's ward they hadn't yet been switched on.

'My mum said you were in the paper this morning!' A bright little five-year-old sang out as Annika did her obs.

'What's "allegedly" mean?' asked another.

'Why don't you change your name?' asked Luke as she took down his dressing just before she was due to finish. Ross wanted to check his leg ulcer before it was re-dressed, and Annika was pleased to see the improvement. 'Then no one would know who you are.'

'I've thought about it,' Annika admitted. 'But the papers would make a story out of that too. Anyway, whether I like the attention or not, it is who I am.'

His dressing down, she covered his leg with a sterile sheet and then checked off on his paperwork before the end of her shift.

'What's your blood sugar?'

'Dunno.'

It had been a long day for Annika, and maybe her own tact button was on mute for now, but she was tired of reasoning with him, tired of the hourly battles when it was really simple. 'You know what, Luke? You can argue and you can kick and scream and make it as hard as you like, but why not just surprise everyone and do it for yourself? You say you want your mum to leave you alone, to stop babying you—maybe it's time to stop acting like one.'

It was perhaps unfortunate that Ross came in at that moment.

'His dressing's all down,' Annika gulped.

'Thanks. I'll just have a look, and then you can re-dress.'

'Actually, my shift just ended. I'll pass it on to one of the late staff.'

She turned to go, but Ross was too quick for her.

'If you could wait in my office when you've

finished, Annika,' Ross said over his shoulder. 'I'd like a quick word.'

Oh, she was really in trouble now.

She hadn't been being mean—or had she?

Maybe she should have been more tactful with Luke…

She couldn't read Ross's expression when he came in.

He was dressed in a suit, even though he hadn't been in one this morning, and he looked stern and formidable. Unusually for Ross, he also looked tired, and he gave a grim smile when she jumped up from the chair at his desk.

'Is Luke okay?'

'He's fine. I asked Cassie to do his dressing.'

'Was he upset?'

'Upset?'

'Because I told him he should be taking his own blood sugars?'

'He just took it.'

'Oh.'

Ross frowned, and then he shook his head in

bewilderment. 'Do you think you're here to be told off?'

'I told him he was acting like a baby.'

'I've told him the same,' Ross said. 'Many times. You were fine in there—would you please stop doubting yourself all the time?'

'I'll try.'

'How come you're finishing early?'

'I worked through lunch; I'm going home at three.' She let out a breath. 'It's been a long day.'

'That offer's still there.' He saw her slight frown. 'To talk.'

'Thank you.'

And when she didn't walk off, neither did Ross.

'Do you want to come riding?' There was an argument raging in his head—he was going away soon, they had promised to keep things on ice till he returned, and yet he couldn't just leave her like this.

'Riding?'

'At the farm.'

'I've never ridden.'

'It's the best thing in the world after a tough day,' Ross said. 'You'll love it.'

'How do you know?' Annika said.

'I just know.' He watched her cheeks darken further. 'Annika, I will not lay a finger on you. It's just a chance to get away...'

'I don't like talking like this when I'm on duty.'

'Then give me half an hour to call in a favour and I'll meet you in the canteen.'

She *wasn't* going back to the farm with him. Her hand was shaking as she opened her locker, and then she picked up her phone and turned it on. She saw missed calls from her mother, her family's agent, her brother Iosef, a couple from Annie and four from Aleksi. She turned it off. Right now she was finding it very hard to breathe.

She didn't want to go home.

Didn't want to give a comment.

Didn't want a spin doctor or a night out at some

posh restaurant with her family just to prove they were united.

Which was why she turned left for the canteen.

He drove; she followed in her own car. He had a small flat near the hospital, Ross had explained, for nights on call, but home was further away, and by the time they got there it was coming up for five. As they slid into his long driveway, she saw the tumbled old house and sprawling grounds. For the first time since she had been awoken by a journalist at five a.m., asking her to offer a comment, Annika didn't have to remember to breathe.

It just happened.

And when she stepped out of the car she saw all the flowers waving in the breeze—the same kind of flowers he had brought for her.

Ross *had* picked them.

The inside was scruffy, but nice: boots in the hallway, massive couches, and a very tidy kitchen, thanks to the cleaner who was just leaving.

'Hungry?' Ross asked, and she gave a small shrug.

'A bit.'

'I'll pack a picnic.'

'Am I to learn to ride in my uniform?'

He laughed and found her some jodhpurs that he said belonged to one of his sisters, some boots that belonged to someone else, though he wasn't sure who, and an old T-shirt of his.

Annika didn't know what she was doing here.

But it was like a retreat and she was grateful for it.

She was grateful too for familiarity in the strangest of places. There were pictures of Iosef there with Ross, from twenty years old to the present day. They grew up before her eyes as she walked along the hallway—and, though she had never really discussed the Detsky Dom with her brother, somehow with Ross she could.

'I expected them to be more miserable,' Annika said, staring at a photo of some grinning, pimply-faced teenagers, with Ross and Iosef beaming in the middle. It was a Iosef she had never seen.

'Our soccer team had just won!' Ross grinned at the memory. 'It's not all doom and gloom.'

'I know,' Annika said, glad that now she did, because there were so many questions she felt she couldn't ask her brothers.

'There's an awful lot of love there,' Ross said, 'there's just not enough to go around. The staff are wonderful…'

And she was glad to hear that.

She was glad too when she walked back into the kitchen. They had had very little conversation—she was too tired and confused and brain-weary to talk—but he got one essential thing out of the way.

He held her.

It was as if he had been waiting for her, and she stepped so easily into his arms. She never cried, and she certainly wouldn't now, but it had been a horrible day, a rotten day, and although Iosef, Annie, Aleksi, her friends, would all do their best to offer comfort—she was sure of that—Ross was far nicer. He didn't ask, or make her explain, he just held her, and the attraction that had always been there needed no explanation or discussion. It just was. It just *is*, Annika thought.

His chest smelt as she remembered. He was, she decided as she rested in his arms, an absolute contradiction, because he both relaxed and excited her. She could feel herself unwind. She felt the hammer of his heart in her ear and looked up.

'One kiss,' she said.

'Look where that got us last time.'

'Just one,' Annika said, 'to chase away the day.'

So he kissed her. His lovely mouth kissed hers and her wretched day disappeared. He tasted as unique as he had the first time he'd kissed her, as if blended just for her. His mouth made hers an expert. They moved as if they were reuniting, tongues blending and chasing. His body was taut, and made hers do bold things like press a little into him. Her fingers wanted to hook into the loop of his belt and pull him in harder, and so she did. Their breathing was ragged and close and vital, and when he pulled back he gave her that delicious smile.

'Come on.'

He gave her his oldest, slowest, most trustworthy horse to ride, and helped her climb on, but even as the horse moved a couple of steps she felt as if the ground was giving way and let out a nervous call.

'Sit back in the saddle.' Ross grinned. 'Just relax back into it.'

She felt as if she would fall backwards, or slide off, every muscle in her body tense as they clopped at a snail's pace out of the stables.

'Keep your heels down,' Ross said, as if it were that easy. Every few steps she lost a stirrup, but the horse, along with Ross, was so endlessly patient that soon they were walking. Annika concentrated on not leaning forward and keeping her heels down, and there was freedom, the freedom of thinking about nothing other than somehow staying on. After a little while Ross goaded her into kicking into a trot.

'Count out loud if it helps.' He was beside her, holding his own reins in one hand as she bumped along. It was *exciting* for maybe thirty seconds, as she found her rhythm and then lost it. She pulled on the reins to stop, and then the only thing Annika could do was laugh. She laughed with a strange freedom, exhilaration ripping through her, and Ross was laughing too.

'Better?'

'Much.' She was breathless—from laughing, from riding, from dragging in the delicious scent of dusk, and then, when she slid off the horse and he spread out a picnic, she was breathless from just looking at him.

'It helped,' Annika said. 'You were right.'

'After a bad day at work,' Ross said, 'or a difficult night, this is what I do and it works every time.' He gave her a smile. 'It worked for me today.'

'Was today a bad day?' Annika asked, and he looked at her.

'Today was an exceptionally bad day.'

'Really?' She cast her mind back. Was there something she had missed on the ward? An emergency in ICU, perhaps?

But Ross smiled. 'I had a meeting with the CEO!'

'I wondered what was with the suit.'

'On my return they want me to commit to a three-year contract. So far I have managed to avoid it...'

'Does a three-year contract worry you?'

'More the conditions.' He gave a tight smile. 'I'm a good doctor, Annika, but apparently wearing a suit every day will make me a better one.'

'At least it's not an apron,' she joked, but then she was serious. 'You *are* a good doctor—but why would you commit if you are not sure it is what you want?'

And never, not once, had he had that response.

Always, for ever and always, it had been, 'It's just a suit. What about the mortgage? What if...?'

'I love my job,' Ross said.

'Do you love the kids or the job?' Annika checked, and Ross smiled again. 'There will always be work for you, Ross.'

'I've also been worrying about you.'

'You don't have to worry about me.'

'Oh, but I do.'

They ate cold roast beef and hot mustard sandwiches and drank water. The evening was so still and delicious, so very relaxing compared to the drama waiting for her at home.

'I should get back...' She was lying on her back, staring up at an orange sky, inhaling the scent of grass, listening to the sounds of the horses behind them. Ross was so at ease beside her—and she'd never felt more at home with another person.

She looked over to him, to the face that had taken her breath away for so long now, and he was there, staring back and smiling.

A person, Annika reminded herself, who barely knew her—and if he did...

If she closed her eyes, even for a moment, she

knew she would remember his kiss, knew where another kiss might lead, right here, where the air was so clear she could breathe, the sky so orange and the grass so cool.

'I should get back,' she said again. She didn't want to, but staying would be far too dangerous.

'You don't have to go,' Ross said.

'I think I do,' was her reluctant reply. 'Ross, it's too soon.'

'Annika, you are welcome to stay. I'm not suggesting a weekend of torrid sex.' Low in her stomach, something curled in on itself. 'Though of course...' he grinned '...that can be an optional extra...' And then he laughed, and so too did she. 'There's a spare room, and you're more than welcome to use it. If you want a break, a bit of an escape, here's the perfect place for it. I can go and stay at the flat if you prefer...'

'You'd offer me your home?'

'Actually, yes!' Ross said, surprised at himself, watching as she turned on her phone again and winced at the latest flood of incoming messages.

'Hell, I can't imagine what you have to go home to.'

'A lot,' Annika admitted. 'I have kept my phone off all day.'

'You can keep it off all weekend if you like.'

Oh, she could breathe—not quite easily, but far more easily than she had all day.

'I don't want to stay here alone.'

'Then be my guest,' he said.

'I have a shift at the nursing home tomorrow night.'

'I'm not kidnapping you—you're free to come and go,' Ross replied, and after a moment she nodded.

'I'd love to stay, but I should let Aleksi know.'

She rang her brother, and Ross listened as she checked if he was okay and reassured him that she was fine.

'I'm going to have my phone off,' Annika said. 'Tell Mum not to worry.'

He busied himself packing up the picnic, but he saw her run a worried hand through her hair.

'No, don't—because I'm not there,' she said. 'I'm staying with a friend.' She caught his eye. 'No, I'd rather not say. Just don't worry.'

She clicked off her phone and stood. Ross called the horses, and they walked them slowly back.

'It's nice,' Annika said. 'This...' She looked over to him. 'Do your grandparents have horses?'

'They do.'

And he'd so longed for Spain, longed for his native land, yearned to discover all that had seemed so important, so vital, but right now he had it all here, and the thought of Spain just made him homesick.

Homesick for here.

It was relaxing, settling the horses for the night, then heading back to his house.

'Have a bath,' Ross suggested.

'I have nothing to change into. Maybe I should drive back and pack. I haven't got anything.'

'You don't need anything,' Ross said. 'My sisters always leave loads of stuff—they come and stay with the kids some weekends when I'm on call.' He went upstairs and returned a few moments later with some items of clothing and a large white towelling robe. 'Here.' He handed her a toothbrush. 'Still in its wrapper—you're lucky I did a shop last week.'

'Very lucky.'

'So now you have no excuse but to relax and enjoy.'

He poured her a large glass of wine and told her to take it up to the bath, and then he showed her the spare room, which had a lovely iron bed with white linen.

'You have good taste.'

'Spanish linen,' Ross said, 'from my grandmother… She's the one who has good taste.' On the way to the bathroom he kicked open another door. 'I, on the other hand, have no taste at all.'

His bedroom was far more untidy than his office, with not a trace of crisp linen in sight. It was brown on black, with boots and jeans and belts, a testosterone-laden den, with an unmade bed and a massive music system.

'This reminds me of Luke's room.'

'You can come in with your bin liner any time,' Ross said. 'My door is always open...' Then he laughed. 'Unless family's staying.'

The bathroom was lovely. It had a large freestanding bath that took for ever to fill, a big mirror, and bottles of oils, scents and candles.

His home confused her—parts looked like a rustic country home, other parts, like his bedroom, were modern and full of gadgets. It was like Ross, she thought. He was doctor, farmer, gypsy—an eclectic assortment that added up to one incredibly beautiful man.

Settling into the warm oily water, she could, as she lay, think of no one, not one single other person, whose company could have soothed her tonight.

His home was like none she had ever been in.

His presence was like no other.

She washed out her panties and bra, but stressed for a moment about hanging them over the taps to dry. They were divine: Kolovsky silk in stunning turquoise. In fact all her underwear was divine—it was one of the genuine perks of being a Kolovsky. It was seductive, suggestive, and, Annika realised, she could *not* leave it in the bathroom!

So she hung it on the door handle in her bedroom and then headed downstairs, where he sat, boots on the table, strumming at a guitar, a dog looking up at him. She thought about using her fingers as castanets and dancing her way right over to his lap, but they'd both promised to be good.

'Why would you do this for me?' She stood at the living room door, wrapped in his sister's dressing gown, and wondered why she wasn't nervous.

'Because my life's not quite complicated enough,' Ross said, with more than a dash of sarcasm. 'Just relax, Annika, I'm not going to pounce.'

So she did—or she tried to.

They watched a movie, but she was so acutely aware of the man on the sofa beside her that frankly her mother would have been more relaxing company. When she gave in at eleven and went to bed, it was almost frustrating when he turned and gave her a very lovely kiss, full on the lips, that was way more than friendly but absolutely going nowhere. It was, Annika realised as she climbed the steps, a kiss goodnight.

She could taste him on her lips.

So much so that she didn't want to remove the toothbrush from its wrapper. But she did, and she brushed her teeth, and then when she heard him coming up the stairs she raced to her bedroom. She slipped off her dressing gown and slid naked into bed, then cursed that she hadn't been to the loo.

He was filling the bath.

She could hear it, so she decided to make a quick dash for it, but she came out to find him walking down the landing wearing only a black towel round his loins. His body was delicious, way better than her many imaginings, and his hair looked long, and his early-morning shadow was a late-night one now. She just gave a nod.

'Feel free...' He grinned at her awkwardness.

'Sorry?'

'To wash your hands...'

'Oh.'

So she had to go into the bathroom, where his bath was running, as he politely waited outside. She washed her hands and tried not to look at the water and imagine him naked in it.

'Night, Annika.'

'Night.'

How was she to sleep? He was in the bath for ever, and then she heard the pull of the plug and the lights ping off. She lay in the dark silence and knew he was just metres away. And then, just as she thought she might win, as a glimpse of sleep beckoned, she heard music.

There was no question of sleeping here in a strange house, with Ross so close. She couldn't sleep, so instead she did a stupid thing—she checked her phone.

Even as she turned it on it rang, and foolishly she answered. She listened as her mother demanded that she end this stupidity and come home immediately—not to the flat, but home, where she belonged. She was wreaking shame on her family, and her father would be turning in his grave. Annika clicked off the phone, her heart pounding in her chest, and headed out for a glass of water.

The low throb of music from his room somehow beckoned, and his door was, as promised, open. She glanced inside as she walked past.

'Sorry.'

'For what?'

'I'm just restless.'

'Get a drink if you want…' He was lying in the bed reading, hardly even looking up.

'I'll just go back to bed.'

'Night, then.'

She just stood there.

And Ross concentrated on his book.

His air ticket was his bookmark. He'd done that very deliberately—ten days and he was out of here; ten days and he would be in Spain. And then, when he returned—well, then maybe things could be different.

'Night, Annika.'

She ignored him and came and sat on the bed. They kept talking. And it was hard to talk at two a.m. without lying down, so she did, and even with her dressing gown on it was cold. So she went under the covers, and they talked till her eyes were really heavy and she was almost asleep, and then he turned out the light.

'The music...'

'It will turn itself off soon.'

She turned away from him; there were no curtains on the window, just the moon drifting past, and he spooned right into her. She could feel his stomach in her back, and the wrap of his arms, and it was sublime—so much so that she bit on her lip. Then he kissed the back of her head, pulled her in a little bit more, and she could feel every breath he took. She could feel the lovely tumid length of him, and just as she braced herself for delicious attack, just as she wondered how long it would be polite to resist, she felt him relax, his breathing even, as she struggled to inhale.

'Ross, how can you just lie there…?' He wasn't even pretending; he really was going to sleep!

'Relax,' he said to her shoulder. 'I told you, nothing's going to happen—I had a *very* long bath.'

And she laughed, on a day she had never thought she would, on a day she had done so many different things. She lay in bed and counted her firsts: she had been cuddled, and she had hung up the phone on her mum.

The most amazing part of it all, though, was that for the first time in ages she slept properly.

CHAPTER ELEVEN

IT WAS midday when she woke up.

Annika never overslept, and midday was unthinkable, but his bed was so comfortable, and it held the male scent of him even though he had long since gone. Instead of jumping guiltily out of bed she lay there, half dozing, a touch too warm in her dressing gown, smiling at the thought that there was really no point getting up as she had nothing to wear—and there was no way she was getting on a horse today!

She hurt in a place she surely shouldn't!

'Afternoon!' He pushed the bedroom door open, and the door to her heart opened a little wider too. He hadn't shaved, and looked more gypsy-like, dark and forbidden, than she had ever seen him, but he was holding a tray and wearing a smile that she was becoming sure was reserved solely for her. She smiled back at him.

'What did I do to deserve breakfast in bed?'

'You didn't snore, which is very encouraging,' he said, waiting till she sat up before placing a tray on her lap, 'and it's actually *lunch* in bed.'

It was *the* nicest lunch in the world: omelette made from eggs he had collected that morning, with wild mushrooms and cheese. The coffee was so strong and sweet that if she had given orders to the chef at her mother's home he could not have come up with better.

'You're yesterday's news, by the way,' Ross said. 'In case you were wondering.'

She had been.

'Lucky for you some bank overseas has gone into liquidation and the papers have devoted four pages to it—you don't even get a mention.'

'Thank you.'

She had finished her lunch, and he took the tray from her, but instead of heading off he put it on the floor and lay on top of the bed beside her.

'I like having you here.'

'I like being here.'

She could feel his thigh through the sheet. She felt so safe and warm and relaxed, in a way she never would have at the movies with him, or across the table in some fancy restaurant—so much so that she could even get up and go to the loo, brush her teeth and then come to the warm waiting bed.

'I am being lazy,' Annika said as she crossed the room.

'Why not?' Ross said. 'You have to work tonight.'

And he might never know how nice that sentence was—for surely he could never understand the battle of wills, the drama it entailed, merely for her to work.

Ross accepted it.

It was warm. The sun was streaming through the window, falling on the crumpled bed. After hot coffee and the omelette, wearing a thick dressing gown under the covers was suddenly making her feel way too hot. She stared at him, wanting to peel her dressing gown off, to stand naked before him and climb in bed beside him. He stared back for the longest time. The air was thick with lust and want, but with patience too.

'Sleep.' He answered the heavy unvoiced question by standing up. He stood in front of her, and she thought he would go, but she didn't want him to.

There was a mire of confusion in her mind, because it was too soon and sometimes she wondered if she was misreading him. What if he was just a very nice guy who perhaps fancied her a little?

And then he answered her fleeting doubt.

His hands untied the knot of her dressing gown, and she stood as he slid it over her shoulders. She saw his calm features tighten a fraction, felt the caress of his gaze over her body and the arousal in the air.

She was naked in front of him, and he was dressed, and yet it felt appropriate. She could not fathom how, but if felt right that he should see her, that they glimpsed the future even if it was too soon to reach for it. She felt safe as he pulled the bedcovers over her.

Only then did he kiss her. He kissed the hollows of her throat, sitting on the bed, leaning over where she lay. He kissed her till she wanted him to lie down beside her again, but he didn't. He kissed her until her hands were in his thick black hair, her body stretched to drag him down, but he didn't lie down. He just kissed her some more, till her breath was as hard and as ragged as his. It was just a kiss, but it brought with it indecent thoughts, because they both explored what they knew was to come. Their faces and lips met, but their minds were meshed too. It was a dangerous kiss, that went on and on as her body flared for him, and then he lifted his head and smiled down.

'Go back to sleep.'

'You are cruel.'

'Very.' He smiled again, and then he left her, a twitching mass of desire, but relaxed too. She had never slept more, never felt more cherished or looked after. The horrors were receding with every hour she spent in his presence.

She slept till seven, and then showered and pulled on her uniform. She made his bed before heading downstairs. He offered her some dinner but she wasn't hungry.

'I need to go home and get my agency uniform, and perhaps...' she blushed a little at her own presumption '...perhaps I should pack a change of clothes for tomorrow.'

'Here.' He handed her a key. 'I lie in on Sunday. Let yourself in.' And he handed her something else—a brown paper bag. 'For your break.'

He had made her lunch—well, a lunch that would be eaten at one a.m., after she had helped to get twenty-eight residents into bed and answered numerous call bells.

She deliberately didn't look inside until then. She sat down in the staffroom and took the bag out of the fridge and opened it as excited as a kid on Christmas morning.

He had made her lunch!

A bottle of grapefruit juice, a chicken, cheese and salad sandwich on sourdough bread, a small bar of chocolate and, best of all, a note.

Hope you are having a good shift.
R x
PS I am no doubt thinking about you. R xx

He *was* thinking of her.

Even though she had slept for most of the day, it had been nice knowing Annika was there, and without her now the house seemed empty and quiet.

He had never felt like this about anyone, of that he was sure.

Gypsy blood did flow in his veins, and it wasn't just his looks that carried the gene. There was a restlessness to him that so many had tried and failed to channel into conventional behaviour.

He didn't feel like that with Annika.

Yet.

Her vulnerability unnerved him, his own

actions sideswiped him—it had taken Imelda months to get a key; he had handed it to Annika without thought.

He was going away in little more than a week, digging deep into his past, thinking of throwing in his job... He could really hurt her, and that was the last thing he wanted to do.

Ross headed upstairs and stepped into his room. He smiled at the bed she had made. The tangled sheets were tucked into hospital corners, his pillows neatly arranged. If it been Imelda it would have incensed him, but it was Annika, and it warmed him instead.

And that worried him rather a lot.

CHAPTER TWELVE

SHE flew through the rest of her shift.

There would be no words of wisdom from Elsie, though.

As Annika flooded the room with light at six the following morning, Elsie stared fixedly ahead, lost in her own little world. And though, as Elsie had revealed, she enjoyed being there, this morning Annika missed her. She would have loved some wise words from her favourite resident.

Instead she propped Elsie up in bed and chatted away to her as she sorted out clothes from Elsie's wardrobe, her stockings, slippers, soap and teeth. Then Annika frowned.

'Drink your tea, Elsie.'

No matter Elsie's mood, no matter how lucid she was, every morning that Annika had worked there the old lady had gulped at her milky tea as Annika prepared her for her shower.

'Do you want me to help you?'

She held the cup to her lips, but Elsie didn't drink. The tea was running down her chin.

'Come on, Elsie.'

Worried, Annika went and found Dianne, the Registered Nurse.

'Perhaps just leave her shower this morning,' Dianne said when she came at Annika's request and had a look at Elsie. Instead they changed her bed, combed her hair, and Annika chatted about Bertie and all the things that made Elsie smile—only they didn't this morning.

Annika checked her observations, which were okay. The routine here was different from a hospital: there was no doctor on hand. There was nothing to report, no emergency as such.

Elsie just didn't want her cup of tea.

It was such a small thing, but Annika knew that it was vital.

* * *

It felt strange, driving home to *someone*.

Strange, but nice.

Since her mother had refused to talk to her about her work since she had supposedly turned her back on her family to pursue a 'senseless' career, Annika had felt like a ball-bearing, rattling around with no resting place, careering off corners and edges with no one to guide her, no one to ask where she was.

It felt different, driving to someone who knew where you had been.

Different letting herself in and knowing that, though he was asleep, if the key didn't go in the lock she would be missed.

She felt responsible, almost, but in the nicest way.

She dropped the bag she had packed on the bathroom floor, and then slipped out of her uniform and showered, using her own shampoo that she had brought from home. It felt nice to see it standing by his shampoo, to wrap herself in his towel and brush her hair and teeth, then put her toothbrush beside his.

The house was still and silent, and she had never felt peace like it.

Nothing like it.

She had never felt so sure that the choice she made now would be right, no matter what it was. The decision was hers.

She could step out of the bathroom and turn right for the spare room and that would be okay.

She could go downstairs and make breakfast and that would be fine too.

Or she could slip into bed beside him and ask for nothing more than his warmth, and that would be the right choice too.

It was her choice, and she was so grateful he was letting her make it.

His door *was* always open, and she stepped inside and stood a moment.

He needed to shave—his jaw was black and he looked like a bandit. His eyes were two slits and she knew he was deeply asleep. He was beautiful, dark and, no doubt—according to her mother—completely forbidden, but he was hers for the taking—and she wanted to take.

Annika slipped in bed beside him, her body cool and damp from the shower, and he stirred for a moment and pulled her in, spooned in beside her, awoke just enough to ask how her shift had been.

'Good.'

And then she felt him fall back to sleep.

His body was warm and relaxed, and hers was cold, tired and weary, drawing warmth from him. She felt him unfurl, felt him harden against her, and then he turned onto his back. She lay there for a moment, till his breathing evened out again, and then she rested her wet hair on his chest and wrapped her cold foot between his warm calves. She slid her hand down to his hardening place, heard his breath held beneath her ear, and turned her head and kissed his flat nipple. Her hand stroked him boldly—because this was no sleepy mistake.

'Annika...'

'I know.' She did—she knew they were

supposed to be taking it slow, knew he was going away, knew it was absolutely bad timing—but…

'I want it to be you.'

'What if…?'

'Then I still want it to be you.'

Her virginity, in that moment, was more important to Ross than it was to her. To him it denoted a commitment that he thought he wasn't capable of making, yet he had never felt more sure in his life.

She traced his lovely length to the moist tip, and then he lifted her head, gently pulled at her hair so that he could kiss her. His hand was on her breast, warming it, holding its weight. Then he was stroking her inside, her warm centre was moist, and she was glad his mouth had left hers because she wanted to bite on her lip.

He kissed her low in the neck, a deep, slow kiss, and he was restraining himself in case he bruised her, but she wanted his bruise, so she pushed at his head, rocking a little against him as his lips softly branded her.

'Put something on,' she begged, because she wanted to part her legs so badly.

'Are you sure?' It was the right thing to say, but it seemed stupid, and Annika clearly thought the same.

'Yes!' she begged. 'Just put something on.'

He was nuzzling at her breasts now, as his fingers still slid inside her, and his erection was there too, heavy on her inner thigh, teasing her as his other hand frantically patted at the bedside drawer.

She was desperate.

Little flicks of electricity showered her body. She was wanton as he suckled at her breast and searched unseeing in the drawer. Then she held him again, because she wanted to. She took his tip and slid it over her, and he moaned in hungry regret because he wanted to dive in. Side by side they explored each other's bodies as still he searched for a condom.

'Here…' He waved it as if he had found the golden ticket, his hand shaking as he wrestled with the foil.

Still she held him, slid him over and over the place he wanted to be till it was almost cruel. He was so hard, so close, and she didn't want him sheathed. She wanted to see and feel—but he had a shred of logic and he used it. He sheathed himself more quickly than he ever had, but he didn't dive in, because he didn't want to hurt her. He claimed her breast again with his mouth, and she cupped him and stroked him again. She teased him, but she could only tease for so long—and then she got her reaction: he was gently in. She was breaking every ingrained rule and it felt divine.

'Did I hurt you?' he checked.

'Not yet.'

And he swore to himself that he wouldn't.

Yes, he'd made that promise more than a few times before, but this time he hoped he meant it.

She wanted more, and he pushed so hard into her that she had to lie back. She wanted to accommodate him, to orientate herself to the new position. Those little flicks of electricity had merged into a surge—she couldn't breathe. He was bucking inside her and she was frantic. She thought she might swear, or cry out his name, but she held back from that. She could feel his rip of release and she wanted to scream, but she wouldn't allow herself. She bit on his shoulder instead, sucked his lovely salty flesh and joined him—*almost.*

Not with total abandon, because she didn't yet know what that was, but she joined him with a rare freedom she had never envisaged.

Then, after, he waited.

As she fell asleep, still he waited.

For the thump of regret, the sting of shame, for him to convince himself that he was just a bastard—but it never came.

CHAPTER THIRTEEN

HE WAS a very patient teacher—and not just in the bedroom. Round and round the field she bobbed, trot, trot, and she even, to her glee, got to gallop. Then Ross showed her the sitting trot, in which her bottom wasn't to lift out of the seat. He did it with no hands, made it look so easy, but it was actually hard work.

Around Ross she was always starving.

'It's all the exercise!'

She laughed at her own little joke and he kissed her. Then, when she wanted so much more than a kiss, very slowly he took off her boots and she lay back. She could feel the sun on her cheeks and the breeze in the trees, and life was, in that moment, perfect. He sorted out her zip and she let him. In everything she was inhibited—at work, with friends, with family—but not with Ross.

In this, with him, there was no fear or shame, just desire.

'There,' she told him, because where he was kissing her now was perfect.

'Again,' she said, when she wanted it there again.

'More,' she said, when she wanted some more.

She pulled his T-shirt over his head, berating him the second his mouth stopped working so it resumed duty again.

She wanted more—and not just for herself, so she pulled at her own T-shirt till all she wore was a bra. Then she didn't care what she was wearing. She could feel his ragged breathing on her tender skin and sensed her pleasure was his.

He was unshaved, and she was tender, so she had to push him back, just once, and yet she so much wanted him to go on.

And he dived in again, but she was still too tender.

So she pulled at his jodhpurs and freed him instead.

He was divine, his black curls neat and manicured, the erection glorious and dark, so that she had to touch. Her fingers stroked, guided, and he was there at her entrance, moistening it a little. It was so fierce to look at, yet on contact more gentle than his lips.

'Please...' She was so close to coming she lifted her hips.

'They're in there...' He was gesturing to the backpack, a lifetime away, or more like ten metres, but it was a distance that was too far to fathom. He might just as well have left the condoms in the bathroom.

It was the most delicious tease of sex to come. He was stroking against her and she was purring, her hips rising, begging that he fill her and for it not to stop.

'Just a little way...' Her voice was throaty, and he stared down at her, so pink and swollen. How could he not? He entered her just a little.

He was kneeling up, holding her buttocks, and

his eyes roamed her body. He thought he would come. She was all blonde and tumbled, and in underwear that would make working beside her now close to impossible, because if he even pictured her in that… He pushed it in just a little bit more as Annika—shy, guarded Annika—gave him a bold, wanton smile that had his heart hammering. He pulled down the straps on her bra and freed her breasts, and she boldly took his head and led him there. She kissed his temple as he suckled her. He moved within her till he wanted more than just a little way, and so too did she.

He leant back and guided her, up and down his length. She had never felt more pliant, moving as his hands guided her. She could see his dark skin against her paleness, and she felt as if she were climbing out of her mind and watching them, released from inhibition. She cried out, could see her thighs trembling, her back arching. Then she climbed back into her body and felt the deep throb of an orgasm that didn't abate. It swelled and rolled like an ocean, took away her breath and dragged her under, and she said his name, thought she swore. Still he was pounding within her, so fast and hard that even as her orgasm faded she thought it would happen again.

And it did—because he was mindful. Just as he satisfied her he gave in, pulled out of her warmth and shivered outside her. She watched. It was startling and beautiful and intimate.

Their intimacy shocked her.

It shocked her that this was okay, that *they* were okay, that they could do all that and afterwards he could just pull her to him.

They lay for a long time in delicious silence, and all Ross knew was that they had completely crossed a line—it wasn't about condoms, or trips to Spain, or families, or all things confusing.

It was, in that moment, incredibly simple.

They were both home.

CHAPTER FOURTEEN

'YOU might want to get dressed...' They were both half dozing when Ross heard the crunch of tyres. 'I think we've got visitors.'

And, though they were miles from being seen, Annika was horrified. As she dressed quickly Ross took his time and laughed. She tripped over herself pulling on her jodhpurs.

'No one can see,' he assured her.

'Who is it?'

'My family, probably...' Ross said, and then there were four blasts of a horn, which must have confirmed his assumption because he nodded. 'There's no rush; they'll wait.'

'I'll go home.' Annika was dressed now. The horses were close by, and she would put up with *any* pain just to make it to the safety of her car. 'I'll just say a quick hello and then go.'

'Don't rush off.' For the first time ever he looked uncomfortable.

'What will they think, though?' Annika asked, because if *her* mother had turned up suddenly on a Sunday evening to find a man at her home she would think plenty—and no doubt say it too.

'That I've got a friend over for the afternoon,' Ross said, but she knew he was uncomfortable.

As they rode back her heart was hammering in her chest—especially when another car pulled up and several more Wyatt family members piled out. His father was very formal, his sisters both much paler in colouring than Ross, and his mother, Estella, was raven-haired and glamorous. Grandchildren were unloaded from the car. His sisters said hi and bye, and relieved them of their horses before heading out for a ride in what was left of the sun.

'Hi, Imelda!'

The sun must have gone behind a cloud, because it was decidedly chilly.

'This is Annika,' Ross said evenly. 'She's a friend from the hospital. Iosef's sister...'

'Oh, my mistake.' His mother gave a grim smile. 'It's just with the blonde hair, and given that she's wearing Imelda's things, you'll forgive me for being confused.'

Ross's brain lurched, because never before had his mother shown her claws.

She had never been anything other than a friend to him, but now she was stomping inside. A row that had never before happened between them was about to start—and it was terrible timing, because he had to deal with Annika as well.

'Imelda?'

'My ex,' Ross said.

'How ex?'

'A few weeks.'

And she wasn't happy with that, so she demanded dates and he told her.

'Was there time to change the sheets?'

'Annika, I never said I didn't have a past.'

'And I'm standing here dressed in her things!'

'It's not as bad as it sounds…'

'It's worse,' Annika said. 'Can you get my keys?'

'Don't go.'

'What—do you expect me to go in and make small talk with your family? Can you please go and get my things?'

It was like two patients collapsing simultaneously at work. Two blistering things he had to deal with.

Annika refused to bend—she wanted her keys and no more.

Ross stomped into the house.

'What the hell?' His voice was a roar. 'How *dare* you do that to her?'

'She'll thank me!' Estella shouted. 'And don't, Reyes—don't even try to justify it to me. "I've got to sort myself out." "I want to find myself." "I'm not getting involved with anyone…"' She hurled back everything he had said, and then she called him a *cabrón* too! He vaguely remembered it meant a bastard. 'I had Imelda on the phone last night, and again this morning. You shred these girls' hearts and we're supposed to say *nothing*?'

'Annika's different!'

'Oh, it's *different* this time, is it?' Estella shouted, and the windows were open, so Ross knew Annika could hear. 'Because apparently you said that to Imelda too!'

And then she really let him have it.

Really!

She called him every name she could think of. Later, Ross would realise that she had probably been talking to Reyes senior. Every bit of hurt his biological father had caused his mother, all the shame, anger and fury that had never come out, had chosen that afternoon to do so.

And his time was up. Annika was storming through the house, finding her keys for herself as his mother continued unabated.

Ross raced out behind her to the car.

'It's not that bad...'

'Really?' Annika gave him a wide-eyed look as she turned the key in the ignition. 'From the sounds inside your home, you're the only who thinks that way.'

'You're just going to drive off…?' He couldn't believe it. He didn't like rows, but he didn't walk away from them either. 'All that's happened between us and you'll just let it go…?'

'Watch me!' Annika said, and she did just that. She gunned the car down his drive, still dressed in Imelda's things. His mother's words about her own son still ringing in her ears.

It was only when she went into her flat, kicked off her boots and ripped off those clothes that she calmed down.

Well, she didn't calm down, exactly, but she realised it wasn't that she had been wearing Imelda's things, or what his mother had said, or anything straightforward that had made her so angry. It was that, just like her family, he had fed her a half-truth.

And, as she had with her family, she had been foolish enough to trust him.

CHAPTER FIFTEEN

ELSIE was right—you should never let the sun go down on a row, because as the days moved on life got more complicated. It was cold and lonely up there on her high horse, and next Tuesday Ross flew out to Spain. More importantly, her midway report on her time with the children's ward was less than impressive, and she was considering the very real good she could do working on the family foundation board.

She wanted his wisdom.

She attempted a smile, even tried to strike up a conversation. She finally resorted to wearing the awful wizard apron that always garnered comment. But Ross didn't bat an eye.

Because Ross was sulking too.

Yes, he'd messed up, but the fact that she hadn't let him explain incensed him. His mother, two minutes after Annika had left, had burst into tears, and George had had to give her a brandy.

Then George, who had always been a touch lacking in the emotion department, had started to cry and revealed he was dreading losing his son!

Ross had problems too!

So he ignored her—wished he could stop thinking about her, but ignored her.

Even on Saturday.

Even as she left the ward, still he didn't look up.

'Enjoy the ball!' Caroline called. 'You can tell us all about it tomorrow.'

'I will,' Annika said. 'See you then.'

He could feel her eyes on the top of his head as he carried on writing his notes.

'See you, Ross.'

Consultants didn't need to look up; he just gave her a very clipped response as he continued to write.

'Yep.'

Annika consoled herself that this was progress.

* * *

'You're not working this afternoon, are you?' Dianne frowned as Annika came into the office.

'No,' Annika said. 'I just popped in to check my roster.'

It was a lie and everyone knew it. She wasn't due for a shift for another week, and anyway she could have rung to check. She had, to her mother's disgust, worked on the children's ward this morning, but they had let her go home early. Instead of taking advantage of those extra two hours, and racing to her mother's to have her hair put up and her make-up applied for the ball, she'd *popped in to check her roster.*

'How's Elsie?' Annika asked. 'I rang yesterday and the GP was coming in…'

'She's not doing so well, Annika,' Dianne said. 'She's got another UTI, and he thinks she might have had an infarct.'

'Is she in hospital?'

'She's here,' Dianne said, 'and we're making her as comfortable as we can. Why don't you go in and see her?'

Annika did. Elsie wasn't particularly con-fused, but she didn't recognize Annika out of uniform.

'Is any family coming?' Annika asked Dianne.

'Her daughter's in Western Australia, and she's seventy,' Dianne said. 'She's asked that we keep her informed.'

Annika sat with Elsie for a little while longer, but her phone kept going off, which disturbed the old lady, so in the end Annika kissed Elsie good-bye and asked Dianne if she could ring later.

'Of course,' Dianne said. 'She's your friend.'

CHAPTER SIXTEEN

STARING out of her old bedroom window, Annika felt the knot in her stomach tighten at the sight of the luxury cars waiting lined up in the driveway.

She could hear chatter and laughter downstairs and was loath to go down—but then someone knocked at the door.

'Only me!' Annie, her sister-in-law, popped her head round and then came in. 'You look stunning, Annika.'

'I don't feel it.' She stared in the mirror at the curled blonde ringlets, at the rouge, lipstick, nails and the thousands of dollars worth of velvet that hugged her body and felt like ripping it off.

'But you look gorgeous,' Annie protested.

How did Annie balance it? Annika wondered. She had probably spent half an hour getting ready.

Her dark curls were damp at the ends, and she was pulling on a pair of stockings as she chatted. Her breasts, huge from feeding little Rebecca, were spilling out her simple black dress. And her cheeks had a glow that no amount of blusher could produce—no doubt there was a very good reason why she and Iosef were so late arriving for pre-dinner drinks!

'It's going to be fun!' Annie insisted. 'Iosef was dreading it too, but I've had a fiddle and we're on the poor table.'

'Pardon?'

'Away from the bigwigs!' Annie said gleefully. 'Well, we're not sitting with the major sponsors of the night.'

And then Annie was serious.

'Iosef meant it when he said if you needed a hand.'

'I cashed the cheque.'

'We meant with your studies.' Annie blew her fringe out of her eyes. Iosef's family were all impossible—this little sister too. There was a wall that Annie had tried to chip away at, but she'd never even made a dint. 'I know it must be hell for you now—finding out what your mother did…'

'Had she not…' Annika's blue eyes glittered dangerously '…your beloved Iosef wouldn't be here. Do you ever think of *that* when you're so busy hating her?'

'Annika, please, let us help you.'

'No!' Annika was sick of Annie—sick of the lot of them telling her how she felt. 'I don't need your help. I'm handing in my notice, and you'll get your money back. All my mother did was try and look after her family—well, now it's my turn to look after her!'

She stepped out of the car and smiled for the cameras. She stood with her mother and smiled ever brighter, and then she walked through the hotel foyer and they were guided to the glittering pre-dinner drinks reception.

Diamonds and rare gems glittered from throats and ears, and people sipped on the finest champagne. Annika dazzled, because that was what was expected of her, but it made no sense.

Hundreds of thousands would have been spent on tonight.

Aside from the luxury hotel and the fine catering, money would have been poured into dresses, suits, jewels, hairdressers, beauticians, prizes and promotion. All to support a cluster of orphanages the Kolovskys had recently started raising funds for.

All this money spent, all this gluttony, to support the impoverished.

Sometimes, to Annika, it seemed obscene.

'You have to spend it to make it,' her mother had said.

'Annika...' Her mother was at her most socially vigilant. Everything about tonight had to be perfect. The Kolovskys had to be seen at their very best—and that included the daughter. 'This is Zakahr Belenki, our guest speaker...'

'*Zdravstvujte,*' he greeted her formally, in Russian, and Annika responded likewise, but she was relieved when he reverted to English.

He was a Detsky Dom boy made good—a self-made billionaire and the jewel in the crown that was tonight. He poured numerous funds into this charity, but he was, Zakahr said, keen to raise awareness, which was why he had flown to the other side of the world for this ball.

This, Nina explained, was what tonight could achieve, proof of the good they could do. But though Zakahr nodded and answered politely to her, his grey eyes were cold, his responses slightly scathing.

'I've heard marvellous things about your outreach programme!' Annika attempted.

'What things?' Zakahr asked with a slight smirk, but Annika had done her homework and spoke with him about the soup kitchen and the drop-in centre, and the regular health checks available for the street children. She had heard that Zakahr was also implementing a casual education programme, with access to computers...

'We would love to support that,' Nina gushed, and then dashed off.

'Tell me, Annika?' Zakahr said when they were alone. 'How much do you think it costs to clear a conscience?'

She looked into the cool grey eyes that seemed to see right into her soul and felt as if a hand was squeezing her throat, but Zakahr just smiled.

'I think our support for the education programme is assured,' she said.

He knew, and he knew, and it made her feel sick.

Soon everyone would know, and she could hardly stand it. She wanted to hide, to step off the world till it all blew over, but somehow she had to live through it and be there for her mother too.

'Excuse me…' She turned to go, to escape to the loo, to get away from the throng—except there was no escape tonight, because she collided into a chest and, though she didn't see his face for a second, the scent of him told her that a difficult night had just become impossible.

'Ross.' Annika swallowed hard, looked up, and almost wished she hadn't.

Always she had considered him beautiful; to-night he was devastatingly handsome.

He was in a dinner suit, his long black hair slicked back, his tie knotted perfectly, his shirt gleaming against his dark skin, his earring glittering. His face was, for the first time, completely cleanshaven. She looked for the trademark mockery, except there was none.

'How come…?' She shook her head. She had never for a second factored him into tonight, had never considered that their worlds might collide here.

'I work in the orphanages with your brother.' Ross shrugged. 'It's a very good cause.'

'Of course.' Annika swallowed. 'But…' She didn't continue. How could she? This was her world, and she had never envisaged him entering it.

'I'm also here for the chance to talk to you.'

'There's really not much to say.'

'You'd let it all go for a stupid misunderstanding? Let everything go over one single row?'

'Yes,' Annika said—because her family's

shame was more than she could reveal, because it was easier to go back to the fold alone than to even try to blend him in.

'Hello!' Nina was all smiles. Seeing her daughter speaking to a stranger, she wormed her way in for a rapid introduction, lest it be someone famous she hadn't met, or a contact she hadn't pursued.

'This is my mother, Nina.' Annika's lips were so rigid she could hardly get the words out. 'Mother, this is Ross Wyatt—Dr Ross Wyatt.'

'I work at the hospital with Annika; I'm also a friend of Iosef's.' Ross smiled.

Only in her family was friendship frowned upon; only for the Kolovskys was a doctor, a *working* doctor, considered common.

Oh, Nina didn't say as much, and Ross probably only noticed her smile and heard her twenty seconds of idle chatter, but Annika could see the veins in her mother's neck, see the unbreakable glass that was her mother's eyes frost as she came face to face with the 'filthy gypsy' Iosef had spoken so often about.

She glanced over to Annika.

'You need to work the room, darling.'

So she did—as she had done many times. She made polite conversation, laughing at the right moment and serious when required. But she could feel Ross's eyes on her, could sometimes see him chatting with Iosef, and a job that had always been hard was even harder tonight.

She was the centre of attention, the jewel in the Kolovsky crown, and she had to sparkle on demand.

Just as she had been paraded for the grown-ups on her birthdays as a child, or later at dinner parties, so she was paraded tonight.

Iosef, Aleksi, and later Levander had all teased her, mocked her, because in her parents' eyes Annika had been able to do no wrong. Annika had been the favourite, Annika the one who behaved, who toed the line. Yes, she had, but they just didn't understand how hard that had been.

And how much harder it would be to suddenly stop.

She stood at the edge of the crowd, heard the laughter and the tinkle of glass, felt the buoyant mood, and how she wanted to head over to Ross, to Iosef and Annie, to relax. She almost did.

'Aleksi isn't here…' Her mother's face was livid behind her bright smile, her words spat behind rigid teeth. 'You need to speak to the Minister, and then you need to—'

'I'm just going to have a drink with my friends, with Iosef…'

'Have you *any* idea what people are paying to be here tonight?' Nina said. 'Any idea of the good we can do? And you want to stop and *have a drink*?'

'Annie and Iosef are.'

'You know what I think of *them*. You are better than that, Annika. Your father wanted more for you. Iosef thinks his four weeks away a year helping the orphans excludes him from other duties. Tonight *you* can make a real difference.'

So she did.

She spoke to the Minister. She laughed as his revolting son flirted with her. She spoke fluent

French with some other guests, forgetting that she was a student nurse and that she wiped bums in a nursing home. She shone and made up for the absent Aleksi and she impressed everyone—except the ones that mattered to her the most.

'It's going well!' Annika said, slipping into her seat at their table, putting her hand over her glass when the waiter came with wine. 'Just water, thanks.'

'Ross was just saying,' Iosef started, 'that you're...' His voice trailed off as his mother appeared and spoke in Annika's ear.

'I have to go and sit with them...' Annika said.

'No, Annika, you don't,' Iosef said.

'I want to.' She gave Ross a smile, but he didn't return it.

'It's hard for her,' Annie said, once Annika had gone, but Iosef didn't buy it. He had done everything he could to keep Annika in nursing, and his mother had told him earlier today that Annika was quitting.

'No, she loves this,' he said. 'She always has.'

He looked over to his wife. 'Has she told you that she's handing in her notice at the end of her rotation?'

'Sort of.'

'I told you she wouldn't stick at it.' He glanced at Ross. 'Model, pastry chef, jewellery designer, student nurse...' He looked to where his sister was laughing at something the Minister's son had said. 'I think she's found her vocation.'

Aleksi did arrive. Dinner had already been cleared away, and the speeches were well underway, but because it was Aleksi, everyone pretended not to notice his condition.

A stunning raven-haired beauty hung on his arm and he was clearly a little the worse for wear—and so was she. Their chatter carried through the room, once at the most inappropriate of times, when Zakahr Belenki was speaking of his time in the Detsky Dom.

Abandoned at birth, he had been raised there, but at twelve years of age he had chosen the comparative luxury of the streets. The details were shocking, and unfortunately, as he paused for effect, Aleksi's date, clearly not listening to the speaker, called to the waiter for more wine.

And Ross watched.

Watched as the speaker stared in distaste at Aleksi.

Watched as a rather bored Annika played with her napkin and fiddled with the flower display, or occasionally spoke with her brother's revolting date.

He saw Aleksi Kolovsky yawn as Zakahr spoke of the outreach programme that had saved him.

Clothed him.

Fed him.

Supported him.

Spoke of how he had climbed from the gutters of the streets to become one of Europe's most successful businessmen.

He asked that tonight people supported this worthy cause.

And then Ross watched as for the rest of the night Annika ignored him.

* * *

He'd clearly misread her. Here she was, being how he had always wanted her to be—smiling, talking, dancing, laughing—she just chose not to do it with him.

'Why don't I give you a lift home?'

'There's an after-party event.'

'How about we stay for an hour and then…?'

'It's exclusive,' Annika said.

And he got the point.

Tonight he had seen her enjoying herself in a way that she never had with him.

For once instinct had failed him.

He had been sure there was more, and was struggling to accept that there wasn't.

'It was a good speech from Zakahr…' Ross said, carefully watching her reaction.

'It was a little over the top,' Annika said, 'but it did the job.'

'Is that what this is to you?'

'Ross.' Annika's cheeks were burning. 'You and Iosef are so scathing, but you don't mind spending the funds.'

'Okay.' She had a point, but there was so much more in the middle.

Iosef and Annie were leaving, and they came over and said their goodnights.

'You've got work tomorrow,' Iosef pointed out, when Annika declined a lift from them and said where she was heading.

And then it was just the two of them again, and, though he had no real right to voice an opinion, though she had promised him nothing, he felt as if he had been robbed.

'Are you giving up nursing?'

'Probably,' Annika answered, but she couldn't look at him. Why wouldn't he just leave her? Why, every time she saw him, did she want to fall into his arms and weep? 'Ross, I need to be here for my mother, and there's a good work opportunity for me. Let's face it—I'm hardly nurse of the year. But I haven't properly made up my mind yet. I'm going to finish my paediatric rotation—'

'Come back with me,' Ross interrupted.

How badly she wanted to—to go back to the

farm, where she could breathe, where she could think. Except Ross would be gone on Tuesday, and all this would still be here.

Her mother was summoning her over and Annika took her cue. 'I have to go.'

'I'll see you at work on Monday,' Ross said, and suddenly he was angry. 'If you can tear yourself away from the Minister's son!'

CHAPTER SEVENTEEN

Ross's words rang in her ears as she raced home and pulled on her uniform. After this afternoon, she knew it would confuse Elsie to see Annika in anything else.

Yes, she was supposed to be at the after-party event, and, yes, her mother was furious, but even though she wouldn't get paid for tonight, even though she wasn't on duty, she *had* to be here.

'How is she?' Annika asked, as Shelby, one of the night nurses, let her in.

'Close to the end,' Shelby said. 'But she's lucid at times.'

'Hi, Elsie.'

They were giving her some morphine when Annika walked in, and the smile on the old lady's face was worth all the effort of coming. Now she was in her uniform Elsie recognised her. Yes,

Annika would be tired tomorrow, and, no, she didn't have to be here, but she had known and cared for the old lady for over a year now, and it was a very small price to pay for the friendship and wisdom Elsie had imparted.

'My favourite nurse,' Elsie mumbled. 'I thought you weren't on for a while...'

'I'm doing an extra shift,' Annika said, so as not to confuse her.

'That's good.' Elsie said. 'Can you stay with me?'

She couldn't.

She really couldn't.

She'd only popped in to check on her, to say goodnight or goodbye. She had to be at work at twelve tomorrow. The charity do would be all over the papers—it was unthinkable that she call in sick.

But that was exactly what she did.

She spoke to a rather sour voice on the other end of the phone and said she was getting a migraine and that she was terribly sorry but she wouldn't be in.

There was going to be trouble. Annika knew that.

But she'd deal with it tomorrow. Tonight she had other things to do.

Elsie's big reclining seat was by her bed, and Annika put a sheet over it and sat down beside her. She took the old bony hand in hers and held it, felt the skinny fingers hold hers back, and it was nice and not daunting at all.

She remembered when her father had been so ill. Annie had been his nurse on his final night. How jealous Annika had been that Annie had seemed to know what to do, how to look after him, how to take care of him on his final journey.

Two years on, Annika knew what to do now.

Knew this was right.

It was right to doze off in the chair, to hold Elsie's hand and wake a couple of hours later, when the morphine wore off a little and Elsie started to stir. She walked out to find Shelby.

'I think her medication's wearing off.'

And Shelby checked her chart, and then Elsie's, and agreed with Annika's findings.

Gently they both turned Elsie, and Annika combed her hair and swabbed her mouth so it tasted fresh, put some balm on her lips. Elsie was lucid before the medicine started to kick in again.

'How's Ross?' Elsie asked.

'Wonderful,' Annika said, because she knew it would make Elsie happy.

'He's good to you?' the old lady checked.

'Always.'

'You can be yourself?'

And she should just say yes again, to keep Elsie happy, but she faltered.

'Be yourself,' Elsie said, and Annika nodded. 'That's the only way he can really love you.'

The hours before dawn were the most precious.

Elsie slept, and sometimes Annika did too, but it was nice just to be there with her.

'I'm very grateful to you,' Elsie said, her tired eyes meeting Annika's as the nursing home started to wake up. The hall light flicked on and the drug trolley clattered. 'You're a wonderful nurse.'

Annika was about to correct her, to say she wasn't here as a nurse but as a friend, and then it dawned on her that she could be both. Here, she knew what she was doing, and again Elsie was right.

She *was*, at least to the oldies, a wonderful nurse.

'I'm very grateful to you too,' Annika said.

'For what?'

'You've worked it out for me, Elsie.' And she took Bertie's photo and gave it to Elsie, who held it instead of Annika's hand.

The next dose of morphine was her last.

Annika stepped out into the morning without crying. Death didn't daunt her, it was living that did, but thanks to Elsie she knew at least something of what she was doing.

Her old friend had helped her to map out the beginnings of her future.

CHAPTER EIGHTEEN

'ANNIKA.' Caroline had called her into the office immediately after handover. 'I appreciate that you have commitments outside of nursing, and I know that your off-duty request got lost, but I went out of my way to accommodate you. I changed your shift to a late and you accepted it!'

'I thought I would be able to come in.'

'Your photo is in the paper—dining with celebrities, drinking champagne...' Caroline was having great trouble keeping her voice even. 'And then you call at four a.m. to say you're unable to come in. Even this morning you're...' Her eyes flicked over Annika's puffy face and the bags under her eyes. 'Do you even want to be here, Annika?'

Just over twenty-four hours ago her answer

would have been very different. Had it not been for Elsie, Annika might well have had her notice typed up in her bag.

But a lot had changed.

'Very much so.' Annika saw the dart of surprise in her senior's eyes. 'I have been struggling with things for a while, but I really do want to be here.' Annika was trying to be honest. It wasn't a Kolovsky trait, in fact her life was a mire of lies, but Annika took a deep breath. All she could do was hope for the best. 'I wasn't sick yesterday.'

'Annika, I should warn you—'

'I am tired on duty at times but that is because I have been doing shifts at a private nursing home. Recently I have tried to arrange it so that it doesn't impinge on my nursing time, but on Saturday I found out that my favourite resident was dying. She has no visitors, and I went in to see her on my way home from the party. I ended up staying. Not working,' she added, when Caroline was silent. 'Elsie had become a good friend, and it didn't seem right to leave her. I'm sorry for letting everyone down.'

'Keep us informed in the future,' Caroline said. 'You've got a lecture this morning in the staff-room—why don't you get a coffee?'

She had expected a reprimand, even a written warning. She was surprised when neither came, and surprised, too, when Ross caught up with her in the kitchen.

'Caroline said you were at the nursing home on Saturday night?'

'I'm surprised she discusses student nurses with you.'

'I heard her on the phone to Heather Jameson.'

'Oh.'

'Is that the truth?' He didn't know. 'Or did it take you twenty-four hours to come up with a good excuse?'

'It's the truth.' She filled her mug with hot water.

'So why couldn't you tell me that?' Ross demanded. 'Why did you make up some story about an after-party event?'

'I thought I was just going to drop in on Elsie; I didn't realise that I'd stay the night.'

'You could have told me.'

'And have you tell Caroline?' Annika said. 'Or Iosef? He's given me some money so that I don't have to work there any more.' She swallowed hard. 'I wasn't actually working. I don't expect you to understand, but Elsie has been more than a patient to me, and it didn't seem right to leave her—'

'Hey.' He interrupted her explanations with a smile. 'Careful—you're starting to sound like a nurse.'

'I thought I would be in trouble,' Annika admitted. 'I didn't expect Caroline to understand.'

'You could have told me,' Ross said. 'You could have trusted me...'

'I don't, though,' Annika said.

Her tongue could be as sharp as a razor at times, but this time it didn't slice. He stared at her for a long moment.

'Why do you push everything good away?'

He didn't expect an answer. He was, in fact, surprised when she gave one.

'I don't know.'

Each Monday, patients permitting, one of the senior staff did an informal lecture for the nursing staff, and particularly the students. As they sat in the staffroom and waited for a few stragglers to arrive, Ross struggled to make small talk with the team. His mind was too full of her.

He watched as she came in and took a seat beside Cassie. She smiled to her fellow student, said hello, and then put down her coffee, opened her notebook, clicked on her pen and sat silent amidst the noisy room.

Her eyes were a bit puffy, and he guessed she must have spent the night crying. How he wished he had known—how he wished she had been able to tell him.

Ross waited as the last to arrive took their seats. It was all very informal, even though it was a difficult subject: 'Recognising Child Abuse in a Ward Environment.'

Ross was a good teacher; he didn't need to work from notes. He turned off the television, told everyone to get a drink quickly if they hadn't already. As he talked, he let his eyes roam around the room and not linger on her. She was probably uncomfortable because it was Ross giving the lecture—not that she ever showed it. She nodded and gave a brief smile at something Cassie said, and she glanced occasionally at him as he spoke, but mainly—rudely, perhaps—she looked at the blank television screen or took the occasional note on the pad in her lap.

'Often,' Ross said, 'by the time a child arrives on the ward there is a diagnosis—perhaps from a GP, or Emergency, or perhaps you have a chronically ill child that has been in many times before. It is your responsibility to look beyond the diagnosis, to always remember to keep an open mind.' He glanced around and saw her writing. 'Babies can't tell you what is wrong, and older children often won't. Perhaps they are loyal to their parents, or perhaps they don't even know that something is wrong...'

'How can they not know?' Cassie asked.

'Because they know no different,' Ross said patiently. 'This is particularly the case with emotional abuse, which is hard to define. Neglect is a hard one too. They are used to being neglected. They have grown up thinking this is normal.'

It was a complicated talk, with lots of questions. None from Annika, of course. She just took her notes and sometimes gazed out of the window or down at her hands. Once she yawned, as if bored by the subject, but this time Ross didn't for a moment consider it rude.

He remembered the way she had sat at the charity ball, ignoring the speaker, oblivious to his words. Now, standing in front of everyone, he started to understand.

'A frozen look?' Cassie asked, when he explained what he looked for in an abused child, and Ross nodded.

'You come to recognise it...' he said, then corrected himself. 'Or you sometimes do.'

There were more questions from the floor, and all of a sudden he didn't feel qualified to answer, although he had to.

'These children sometimes present as precocious. Other times,' Ross said, 'they are withdrawn, or lacking in curiosity. You may go to put in an IV and instead of resistance or fear there is compliance, but often there is no one obvious clue...'

He wanted his lecture over; he wanted a moment to pause and think—and then what?

He felt sick. He thought about wrapping things up, but Cassie was like a dog with a bone, asking about emotional abuse—what did he mean? What were the signs?

"Just because I can't see it, I still know you are hurting me."' He quoted a little girl who was now hopefully happy, but had summed it up for so many.

And you either understood it or you didn't, but he watched Annika's mouth tighten and he knew that she did.

'How can you get them to trust you?' another student asked.

'How do you approach them?' Cassie asked.

But Ross was looking at Annika.

'Carefully,' he said. 'Sometimes, in an emergency, you have to wade in a bit, but the best you can do is hope they can trust you and bit by bit tell their story.'

'What if they don't know their story?' Annika asked, her blue eyes looking back at him, and only Ross could see the flash of tears there. 'What if they are only just finding out that the people they love have caused them hurt, have perhaps been less than gentle?'

'Then you work through it with them,' Ross said, and he saw her look away. 'Or you support them as they work through it themselves. It's hard for a child to find out that the people they love, that those who love them—'

'They *can't* love them...' Cassie started. 'How can you say they love them?'

'Yes,' Ross said, 'they can—and that is why it's so bloody complicated.'

He had spoken for an hour and barely touched the sides. He didn't want her to be alone now, he wanted to be with her, but it was never that easy.

'Sorry to break up the party.' Lisa's voice came over the intercom. 'They need you in Emergency, Ross. Two-year-old boy, severe asthma. ETA ten minutes…'

And the run to Emergency would take four.

As everyone dispersed Annika sat there, till it was only the two of them left.

'You have to go.'

'I know.'

Her head was splitting.

Don't tell. Don't tell. Don't tell.

Family.

No one else's business.

How much easier it would be to walk away, to shut him out, to never tell rather than to open her heart?

'You know that my brother, Levander, was raised in the orphanages…'

He did, but Ross said nothing.

'We did not know—my parents said they did not know—but now it would seem that they did.' It was still so hard to believe, let alone say. 'I thought my parents were perfect—it would seem I was wrong. I was told my childhood was perfect, that I was lucky and had a charmed life. That was incorrect too.'

'Annika...'

'You want me to be open, to talk, and to give you answers—I don't know them. When I met my brothers' wives, when I saw what "normal" was, I realised how different my world was...' She shook her head at the hopelessness of explaining something she didn't herself understand. 'I was sheltered, my mind was closed, and now it is not as simple as just walking away. Every day it is an effort to break away. I don't like my mother, and I hate what she did, but I love her.'

'You're allowed to.'

'I realise now my parents are far from perfect. I see how I have been controlled...' She made herself say it. 'How conditional their love actually was. I am starting to see it, but I still want to be able to sustain a relationship with my mother and remember my father with love.'

'I'm sorry.' He had never been sorrier in his life. 'For rushing you, for...'

'It can't be rushed,' Annika said. 'And I am not deliberately not telling you things. Some of it I just don't know, and I don't know how to trust you.'

'You will,' Ross said.

She almost did.

His pager was shrilling, and he had to run to the patient instead of to her. He had to keep his mind on the little boy and, though he was soon sorted, though the two-year-old was soon stable, it was, Ross decided, the hardest patient he had dealt with in his career.

So badly he wanted to speak with her.

CHAPTER NINETEEN

'Hi, Annika?'

'Yes.'

'I'm ringing for a favour.' Now that he understood her a little bit, he could smile at her brusqueness. 'A work favour.'

'What is it?'

'I've got this two-year-old with asthma. Emergency is steaming. There's some poor guy in the next bed after an MVA, and the kid's getting upset.'

'Bring him up, then.'

'The bed's not ready. Caroline says you need an hour,' Ross explained. 'Look, can you ring Housekeeping and ask them…?'

'Just bring him up,' Annika said. 'I'll get the bed ready. Caroline is on her break. It can be my mistake.'

'You'll get told off.'

'I'm sure I will survive.'

'It will be *my* mistake,' Ross said. 'Just make sure the bed's made—that would be great.' He paused for a moment. 'I need another favour.'

'Yes?'

'This one isn't about work.'

'What is it?'

'I'd like…' He was about to say he'd like to talk, but Ross stopped himself. 'I'd like to spend some time with you.'

The silence was long.

'Tonight,' Ross said.

And still there was silence.

'You don't have to talk,' he elaborated. 'We can listen to music…wave to each other…' He thought he heard a small laugh. 'I just want to spend some time with you.'

'I'm busy on the ward at the moment. I don't have time to make a decision.'

She was like no one he had ever met, and she intrigued him.

She would not be railroaded, would not give

one bit of herself that she didn't want to, and he admired her for that. It also brought him strange comfort, because when she had been with him she had therefore wanted to be there— the passionate woman that he had held had been Annika.

He had wanted more than she was prepared to give.

And now he was ready to wait. However long it took for her to trust him.

'He can go up...' Ross said to one of the emergency nurses. 'I've cleared it with the ward.'

The emergency nurse looked dubious, as well she might. The children's ward had made it perfectly clear that it would be an hour at least, but the resuscitation area was busy, with doctors running in to deal with the patient from the car accident, neurologists, anaesthetists... The two-year-old was getting more and more distressed.

He could hear the noise from behind the curtains and gave the babe's mum a reassuring smile, blocking the gap in the curtains just a touch with his body as the toddler and his mother where wheeled out.

'Thanks so much for this.'

'No problem.' He gave her a small grimace. 'They might be a bit put out on the ward when you arrive, but don't take it personally—he's better up there than down here.'

He'd left his stethoscope on the trolley and went over to retrieve it. He considered walking up to the paediatric ward to take the flak, just in case Annika was about to get told off on his account, but then he smiled.

Annika could take it, *would* take it—she had her own priorities, and a blast from Caroline… The smile froze on his face, everything stilled as he heard a colleague's voice from behind the curtain.

'Kolovsky, Aleksi…'

Ross could hear a swooshing sound in his ears as he pictured again the mangled, bloodied body that had been rapidly wheeled past twenty minutes or so ago. His legs felt like cotton wool as he walked back across the resus unit and parted the curtains.

The patient's face had been cleaned up a bit, though Ross wasn't sure he would have recognised him had he not heard his name, but, yes, it was him.

His good friend Iosef's identical twin.

Annika's brother.

'Aleksi…' His voice was a croak and he had to clear it before he continued. 'Aleksi Kolovsky.'

'His sister works here, doesn't she?' A nurse glanced up. 'Annika? One of the students…?'

He stood and watched for a few moments, more stunned than inquisitive. He watched as the powerful, arrogant man he had met just the once extended his arms, indicative of a serious head injury, and grunted with each breath. The anaesthetist had decided to intubate, but just before he did, Ross went over.

'I'm going to get Annika for you,' he said, 'and you're going to be okay, Aleksi.'

CHAPTER TWENTY

THE hospital grapevine worked quickly, and Ross was aware not just that he had to let Annika know, but his good friend Iosef too.

The Kolovskys were famous. It would be breaking news soon—not just on the television and the internet, but the paramedics and emergency personnel would be talking, and both Iosef and his wife Annie worked in another emergency department across the city.

As he walked he scrolled through his phone. He didn't have Annie's number, only Iosef's, but, deciding it would be better for his friend to hear it from his wife, he called their emergency department. He found out that Iosef was just being informed and would be there to see Aleksi for himself shortly.

Ross moved faster, walked along the long

corridor at a brisk pace, bracing himself for Annika's reaction and wondering what it would be.

He spoke briefly with Caroline, informed her of the news he would be imparting, and then headed down to room eleven.

'He's settled.' She was checking the asthma baby's oxygen saturation; he was sleeping now, his mother by his side.

'That's good,' Ross said. 'Annika, could I have a word, please?'

'Of course.' She nodded to the mother and stepped outside. 'There was no trouble with Caroline—the cot was prepared...'

'Thanks for that. Would you mind coming into my office?'

Her eyes were suddenly wary.

'It's a private matter.'

'Then it can wait till after work,' Annika said.

'No, it's not about that...' He blew out a breath, wondered if perhaps he should have taken up Caroline's suggestion and let her be the one to tell Annika, but, no, he wanted it to come from him—however little he knew her, still he knew her best. 'Just come into my office, please, Annika.'

She did as told and stood, ignoring the seat he offered, so he stood too.

'There was a patient brought into Emergency,' Ross said. 'After a motor vehicle accident. It's Aleksi, Annika.'

'Is he alive?'

'Yes.' Ross cleared his throat. 'He's unconscious; he has multiple injuries and is still being assessed.' She was pale, but then she was always pale. She was calm, but then she was mostly calm. She betrayed so little emotion, and for Ross it was the hardest part of telling her. She just took it—she didn't reach out, didn't express alarm. It was almost as if she expected pain.

'I'll tell Caroline that I need to…'

'She knows,' Ross said. 'I'll take you down there now.'

Annika only wavered for a second. 'Iosef…'

'He's been informed and is on his way.'

They walked to Emergency. There was no small talk. He briefed her on the little he knew and they walked in relative silence. A nurse took them to a small interview room and they were told to wait there.

'Could I see my brother?' Annika asked.

'Not at this stage,' the nurse said. 'The trauma team are trying to stabilise him. As soon as we know more, a doctor will be in to speak with you.'

'Thank you.'

And then came Iosef and Annie, and Nina, their mother, who was hysterical. Iosef and Annika just sat there, backs straight, and waited as more and more Kolovskys arrived.

And still there was no news.

A doctor briefly popped in to ask the same questions as a nurse had ten minutes previously—was there any previous medical history that was relevant? Had Aleksi been involved in any other accidents or had any illnesses?

'Nothing!' Nina shouted. 'He is fit; he is

strong. This is his first time sick—please, I need to scc my son.'

And then they went back to waiting.

'Do *we* keep relatives waiting as long as this?' Iosef's patience was finally running out. 'Do they *know* I'm an emergency consultant?'

'I'll ask again,' Annie said.

'I'll come with you.' Ross went with her.

'God!' Annie said, once they were outside, blowing her dark curls to the sky as she let out a long breath. 'I can't stand it in there—I can't stand seeing Iosef...' She started to cry, and all Ross could do was pull a paper towel out of the dispenser and watch as she blew her nose. 'It was the same when his dad died. You know he's bleeding inside, but he just won't say...'

'He will,' Ross said. 'Maybe later—to you.'

'I know.' Annie nodded and forced a smile. 'I should warn you. They're bloody hard work, that family.'

'But worth it, I bet?' Ross said. Then he crossed a line—and he would only do it once. He looked at Annie, and stared till she looked back at him. 'Annika isn't a lightweight.'

'I know she's not.' Annie blushed.

'That family *is* bloody hard work, and Annika's right in the thick of it...'

He watched her cheeks redden further.

'Imagine if you woke up and found out that the grass was red and not green.'

'I don't get you.'

'Imagine if you'd been told all your life how lucky you were, how spoiled and indulged and precious you were, how grateful you should be.'

Annie just frowned.

'Grateful for what?' Ross demanded, and he wasn't sure if he and Annika would make it, because at any moment she was likely to turn tail and run, so he took the opportunity to tell Annie. 'Go and tell your doctor husband, my good friend, to look up emotional abuse. I can't stand the board at the hospital, but maybe on this they're right—there are charities closer to home.

Tell him to wake up and see what's been going on with his own sister.'

He watched her face pale.

'They controlled what she ate, how she spoke, what she thought—have you ever stopped to think how hard it must be to break away from that?'

'We try to help!'

'Not good enough,' Ross said. 'Try harder.'

CHAPTER TWENTY-ONE

THEY could get no information at the nurses' station, so, before Iosef did, Ross pulled rank. He sent Annie back to the relatives' room and walked into resus, past the huddle around the bed, and up to Seb, the emergency consultant, who was also a friend. He was carefully examining X-ray films.

'How's it looking?'

'Not great,' Seb said, 'but there's no brain haemorrhage It's very swollen, though, and it's going to be a while till we know if there's brain damage.'

He was bringing up film after film.

'Fractured sternum, couple of ribs...' Seb was scanning the X-rays and he looked over to Ross, who was scanning them too, looking at the fractures, some old, some new. 'His left leg's a mess, but his pelvis and right leg look clear…' Seb said. The X-rays were just a little harder to read than most. There was an old fracture on Aleksi's right femur, and when he pulled up the chest film Ross looked again and there were a few old fractures there too.

'Any skull fracture?'

'One,' Seb said. 'But, again, it's old.'

'How old?'

'Not sure—there's lots of calcification… The mum says he's never been in hospital. Poor bastard.' Seb cleared his throat. 'Twenty years ago I'd have been calling you.'

'And Social Services,' Ross said, his lips white. 'What happens when it's all these years on?'

'Look, he could have been in an accident they don't know about…' But these fractures were old, and in a child they would have caused huge alarm. 'Let's get him through this first,' Seb said. 'I'll come and talk to the family.'

Nina sobbed through it; the aunts were despairing too. Iosef and Annika just sat there.

Seb was tactful, careful and thorough. He mentioned almost in passing that there were a couple of old injuries, and Nina said he had been in a lot of fights recently, but Seb said no, some looked older. And Iosef remembered a time his brother was ill, the time he came off his bike…

Nina remembered then what had happened.

'Oh, yes…' she said, but her English was suddenly poor, and an aunt had to translate for her.

'Just before the long summer holidays one year he had a nasty tumble. His leg…' she gestured '…his head. But it was nothing too serious.'

Iosef excused himself for some air, and Annika looked at her hands, sometimes at the door, and once or twice at Ross. When he went and sat beside her he gave her hand a little squeeze, and when he started to remove it she held it back. She kept holding it till they moved Aleksi up to ICU.

'Levander's flying over from England,' Iosef said, as he clicked off his phone in yet another waiting room.

'He moved there when he got married,' Annika

explained. 'That is when Aleksi took over the company.'

Her face was as white as chalk, Ross noted. When she came out from seeing her brother, he saw her fingers go to her temples.

'Can you take me home?'

'Of course.'

'Will you tell my mother for me?'

'Of course,' Ross said, though he wasn't particularly looking forward to it. He turned to Nina. 'Annika's not feeling great; I'm going to take her home...'

Nina shot up from her seat. 'You need to be here—for your brother.'

'I am here for my brother,' Annika said. 'But the doctor said it is going to be at least forty-eight hours.'

'If he gets worse...'

'I have said everything I need to to him,' Annika said, and suddenly her eyes held a challenge. 'Have you?'

'You should stay.'

'I can't.'

She was so white he thought she might faint, and he put his arm around her.

'Can you give them the phone number?' she said.

He frowned.

'Your phone number at the farm—my phone battery's flat.'

'I've got Ross's number,' Iosef said, and he gave his sister a small hug. 'Look after her,' he said to Ross.

'I will.'

Ah, but Nina hadn't finished, because Nina hadn't yet got her way. 'If you had any respect for my daughter you would not flaunt this in front of her own mother.'

'I have *so* much respect for your daughter.' It was all he could say, the only way he could respond and remain civil, and it was also true. He had so much respect for Annika—and never more so than now.

A few hours in her mother's company was enough for him.

Annika had had a lifetime.

He took her to his car, held her hair when she threw up in the bin, and then stopped at the all-night chemist for headache tablet and a cold drink too. He promised himself as they drove home in silence that he would never question her, never ask for more than he needed to know, and that if she didn't trust him, then that was okay.

He trusted himself. For the first time he trusted himself with a woman. Trusted that he would do the right thing by her, always, and that one day, he was sure, she would see it.

CHAPTER TWENTY-TWO

'WHAT time's your flight?'

A massive backpack was half filled in the living room, and only then did she remember that he was going to Spain tomorrow. She looked up at the clock and amended that to today.

'It just got cancelled,' Ross said. 'Family crisis.'

'You don't have to do that.' She meant it—she would be okay. She was making decisions for herself, seeing things for herself. She didn't need Ross to get her through this.

'I want to,' Ross said, and though she didn't need him, she *wanted* him.

'You need to find your family.'

'I think I just did.' Ross grinned. 'Heaven help me.'

'She *is* difficult.' Annika had had two headache

tablets and a bath, had refused a cup of coffee and asked for a glass of wine. 'I don't know if I love her, Ross. I am trying to work it out.'

'You will.'

'Can I ask something?' He nodded. 'What do you think will happen with Aleksi?'

'As a doctor, or as a friend?'

'Can you be both?'

'I can try,' Ross said, and he did try. He stood for a full minute, trying to separate the medical from the personal, then trying to put it back together. 'I don't know,' he admitted. 'As Seb said, we won't know for a couple of days yet…' He hesitated, then made himself continue. 'If he can hang in there for a couple of days, that is. He's been unresponsive since they found him. I spoke to him,' Ross said, 'before I came and got you, and I don't know, I can't prove it, it's more gut than brain, but I think he heard…'

He almost hated the hope that flared in her eyes, but what he had said was true. 'I think he was a little bit aware.'

'I want to go to bed.'

'Okay—you have my room. I'll sleep on the couch.'

'Pardon?'

'I've got some explaining to do,' Ross reminded her. 'I was supposed to be apologising about Imelda, the clothes…'

'I accept.' She gave a tight smile. 'If it's okay with you, I would like you to make love to me.'

'Okay…' he said slowly.

'I don't want to think about today,' Annika explained. 'And I know I can't sleep.' Her very blue eyes met his. 'And I'm not really in the mood to talk.' She gave him a very brief smile. 'And you're very good at it.'

'You're a strange girl.'

'I am.'

'Impossible to work out.'

'Very.'

'But I do love you.'

'Then get me through this.'

His love was more than she could fathom right now, its magnitude too much to ponder, yet it was something she accepted—a beautiful revelation that she would bring out and explore later. Right now, she gratefully accepted the gift.

And Ross took loving her very seriously too.

He had never felt more responsible in his life.

He wanted his kiss to right a thousand wrongs, but no kiss was that good, no kiss could. He wanted to show her how much she meant to him.

She couldn't believe she had asked for sex.

Was it wrong?

Should she be sitting with her mother, being seen to do the right thing?

Did she love her brother less because she was not in a room next door?

She was dreading the days that would follow—the pain, the vigil, the hope, the fear—and she knew she had to prepare, to rest, and to get strong for whatever lay ahead.

His kiss made her tremble. It shocked her that even in misery she could be held, kissed, made to feel a bit better, that she could be herself—whoever that was.

He kissed her so deep, slow and even, and when

she stopped kissing him back he kissed her some more. He kissed her face, her neck, and then her breasts, and then he kissed her mouth again.

His bed was a tumble.

There was music, books by the bedside, and a dog scraping on the door down the hall.

But there were coffee beans in the fridge and there would be warm eggs in the morning.

There was a soft welcome any time she wanted it.

And she wanted it now.

He took her away, but he let her come back, and then he took her away again.

She had a fleeting image of being old, of a nurse wheeling her into the shower as she ranted about Ross.

Let me rant.

She coiled her legs around him.

Let me rant about the night when I couldn't survive and I came to his home.

She lost herself in a way she had never envisaged.

She lost herself, and this time she didn't hold

back—she dived into oblivion. She swore she could smcll the bonfire as she felt the magic and the gypsy in him.

He brought her back to a world that was scary, but there was music still playing, and Ross was beside her, and she knew she'd get through. Then she did something she hadn't been able to do at the hospital, that she so rarely did—she cried, and he held her, and it didn't make things better or worse, it just released her.

'I'm sorry about my family.'

She poured it all out, and it probably didn't make much sense, but she said sorry for the past, and the stuff that was surely to come, because Zakahr Belenki knew the truth and so must others. Between gulps she told him that it was only a matter of time, warned him what he was taking on if he was mad enough to get involved with her.

'You don't have the monopoly on crazy families.' Ross grinned. 'Do you remember meeting mine?'

This made her laugh. Then she stared out of the

window and thought about Aleksi. She couldn't be more scared for him if she tried.

'What are you thinking?'

'That you need curtains.'

'He'll be okay.'

'You don't know that.'

But he did.

And so he told her—stuff he had never told anyone.

He told her about intuition, and that some of the stories about gypsies were real, and that, like it or not, she was saddled with someone who was a little bit different too.

CHAPTER TWENTY-THREE

HE WOKE her at six, saw her eyes open with a smile to his, and then the pain cloud them as she remembered.

'No change,' Ross said quickly. 'I just called Iosef.'

'We should go.'

All she had was her uniform, or a suitcase of clothes that belonged to Imelda.

So she settled for his rolled-up black jeans, and a lovely black jumper, and a belt that needed Ross to poke another hole in it—but she did, to her shame, borrow Imelda's boots.

They drove to the hospital. Annika was talking about Annie, how good she had been with her father. It was this that had first made Annika think about nursing. It was a little dot, but it went next to another dot, and then she told him about

Elsie. One day he would join up the complicated dots that were Annika.

Or not.

It didn't change how he felt.

'It's going to be difficult these next weeks,' Annika said as they neared the city. 'Mum will want me to move home. I can just see it...'

'You do what you have to.'

'She's so determined that I give up nursing.'

'What do *you* want, Annika?'

'To finish my training.'

'Then you will.'

They were at the hospital car park now.

'She'll want me there, back in the family business, away from nursing.' They were walking up to ICU. 'I'm so much stronger, but I'm worried that once I'm back there…'

'You've got me now,' Ross said. 'Whatever you need, whatever might help, just say.'

And that helped.

It helped an awful lot.

It helped when they got to the hospital and Nina was so tired that she was the one who had to go home, with a few of the aunties too. Annie was ringing around for a hotel nearby.

'Use my flat,' Ross said, and handed them the keys.

It helped when she kissed him goodbye and went and took her position next to Aleksi and held his hand. She told him he'd better get better. It helped to know that Ross was in the building—that he wasn't at all far away.

Every minute of every day was made better knowing that Ross Wyatt loved her.

CHAPTER TWENTY-FOUR

BEING a doctor brought strange privileges.

It brought insight and knowledge gleaned when a person was at their most vulnerable, and it weighed heavily on Ross. He loved Annika, which meant he cared about Aleksi.

And, he didn't want to keep secrets from Annika, but, like it or not, he knew something that she didn't.

He had spoken with his colleague, Seb, who had revealed that Aleksi had refused any attempt to discuss his past. Ross considered, long into the lonely nights while Annika was at her mother's, if perhaps he should take the easy option and just leave it.

Then one day, checking in on a patient in the private wing of the hospital, Ross saw the Kolovsky clan leaving. The door to Aleksi's room was slightly open. A nurse was checking his obs, but apart from that Aleksi was alone.

Ross walked away, and then turned around and walked back again just as the nurse was going out.

'How are you doing?' He wasn't offended by Aleksi's frown as he attempted to place him—after all, they'd met only once, and Aleksi was recovering from a head injury. 'I was in Emergency when you came in.'

'You'll forgive me if I don't remember, then,' Aleksi said

'I'm also a friend of Annika's; I was at the charity function. Ross Wyatt...'

He shook his hand.

'Annika's spoken about you,' Aleksi said, then closed his eyes and lay back on the pillows. Just as Ross thought he was being dismissed, as he realised the impossibility of broaching the subject of Aleksi's old injuries, Aleksi spoke, though his eyes stayed closed. 'How is Annika doing?'

'Okay.'

'She's moved back home?' Aleksi asked.

'Your mum was upset, with the accident and everything. She wanted Annika close.'

'She should be back at her own flat.' Grey eyes opened. 'Try and persuade her...'

'Annika will be fine,' Ross said, because that much he knew. 'You don't need to worry.'

'For her, I do.'

'Let me do the worrying on that score,' Ross said, and Aleksi gave a small grimace of pain as he tried to shift in the bed. Ross saw his opening. 'That's got to hurt. I saw the X-rays...'

'I'm going to bleep for ever going through security at airports,' Aleksi said. 'I'm full of wires and pins.'

'It was a bit of a mess.'

'So, are you an emergency doctor?'

'No.' Ross shook his head. 'I'm a paediatrician. I was just in Emergency when you came in—and I broke the news to Annika. She asked me to find out more.' He held his breath in his lungs for just a second. 'I was trying to get more information for her. I was speaking to Seb when he was looking over your X-rays.'

'The emergency consultant?' Aleksi checked, and Ross nodded. 'He was up a couple of days ago to see how I was doing.'

And then Aleksi looked at Ross, and Ross looked back, and the conversation carried on for a full two minutes but not a single word was uttered. Finally Aleksi cleared his throat.

'What happens to patient confidentiality if I'm not your patient?'

'You still have it.'

'Even if you're screwing my sister?' Aleksi was savage for a moment, but Ross was expecting it—even if Annika's brother was a generation older than Ross's usual patients, his reaction was not dissimilar.

'I'm a doctor,' Ross said. 'It's my title at home, at work, in bed; it's not a badge I can ever take off. Some conversations with your sister might be more difficult for me—I will have to think hard before I speak, and I will have to remember that I know only what she chooses to tell me—but I'm up to it.'

'Thanks, but no thanks.'

Aleksi closed his eyes and Ross knew he had been dismissed. Inwardly cursing, he turned to go, wondering if he'd made things worse, if he could have handled it better, if he should have just left well alone. And then Aleksi's voice halted him.

'It was only me.'

Ross turned around.

'You don't have to worry that Annika was beaten.' He gave a low mirthless laugh. 'She had it tougher in many ways. My father was the sun, my mother the moon, and they revolved around her. She had the full beam of their twisted love, but they never laid a finger on her. It was just me.'

'I'm sorry,' Ross said, because he was.

'It was my own stupid fault for knowing too much…' He looked up at Ross. 'Every family has their secrets, Ross,' Aleksi said, 'and Levander thinks he knows, and Iosef is sure he knows, but they don't….' He gave a thin smile at Ross's frown.

'Annika told me…' He faltered for a moment. 'Some…'

'About Levander being raised in an orphan-age—and my parents conveniently not knowing he was there?'

Ross nodded.

'That isn't the half of it. And I'll save you from future awkward conversations with my sister by not telling you. Suffice to say I know more than any of them. That's why my father beat me to within an inch of my life, and that's why my mother, instead of taking me to hospital, kept me at home.'

'Any time,' Ross said. 'Any time you can talk to me. And I promise I'll keep it confidential.'

He'd had enough. Ross saw the anger and the energy leave him, knew Aleksi had revealed all that he was going to—for now.

It was almost a relief when Annika walked in, for a quick visit at the end of her shift. She smiled and frowned when she saw Ross with her brother.

'I thought I'd see for myself how he was doing,' Ross said by way of explanation. 'I was just saying to Aleksi that he looks a hell of a lot better than he did last time I saw him.'

'I was wondering why they'd sent a paediatrician to see me.' Aleksi gave a rare smile to his sister. 'I didn't realise at first it was your boyfriend.'

'Boyfriend?' Annika wrinkled her nose. 'He's thirty-two.'

And Ross laughed and left them to it.

He nodded to a colleague in the corridor, chatted to Caroline when he got back to the ward, and then he went into his office and closed the door and sat there.

The cleaner got the fright of her life when she came in to empty the bin and he was still there, in the dark.

'Sorry, Doctor. I didn't realise you were here. Do you want me to turn on the light?'

'No, thanks.'

And he was alone again, in the dark.

With Annika he might always be in the dark.

Might never know the full truth—what she knew, what Aleksi knew… It was like a never-ending dot-to-dot picture he might never be able to join up.

Buena onda. He felt what it meant this time—that vibe, that feeling, that connection. Finally he had it with Annika, and it belonged with Annika.

An ambulance light flashed past and Ross looked around his office. The blue and red lights from the ambulance danced on the walls. He realised he wasn't completely in the dark—there were shades and colour, the glow of the computer, a chink of light under the door, the streetlight outside, the reflective lights of the hospital foyer.

There was light in the dark.

And he didn't have to see it all to know what was there.

He didn't need neat answers, because for Ross there were no longer questions.

There was nothing that could happen, nothing that could be said, nothing that could be revealed that would change how he felt.

More light—his phone glowed as his inbox filled.

And he smiled as he read her meticulous text—no slang for Annika.

My mother just left the building.
I have been told for the last hour how bad
you are for me.
When can we be bad? x

He smiled because everything he wanted and needed he already had—everything she was was enough.

Okay, so she had never said she loved him, and she probably didn't yet fully trust him—but slowly she would.

Ross swore there and then that one day she would, and replied to her text.

ASAP x

CHAPTER TWENTY-FIVE

'Is it possible to request first lunch break?' Annika asked during handover. 'Only, my elder brother is coming from the UK this morning.'

'That shouldn't be a problem,' Caroline said. 'How is Aleksi doing?'

'Better.' Annika nodded. 'A little slower than he would like, but he is improving.'

It had been a tough few weeks.

But full of good times too.

Levander had flown in at the time of the accident and stayed till Aleksi had shown improvement, but had had to return to the UK. Now, though, he was coming with his wife, Millie, and little Sashar for a six-month stay. Levander would take over the running of the Kolovsky empire while Aleksi recuperated. But though it had been wonderful to see Aleksi make such rapid progress, it had been draining too.

Nina had wept and wailed, had made Annika feel so wretched for leaving her alone that she had moved back home. The daily battle just to go to work had begun again.

The control her mother exerted, the secrets of the past, had all sucked her back to a place where she didn't want to be.

The papers had been merciless. It had been proved that neither drugs nor alcohol had been a factor in the accident, but still they had dredged up every photo of Aleksi's wild ways.

And she'd hardly seen Ross.

She'd seen him at work, of course, and they'd managed to go out a couple of evenings, but Nina always managed to produce a drama that summoned her home. Ross had been so patient...

'Oohh, look at you!' Caroline gave a low wolf-whistle as Ross walked past, and Annika gave a rare laugh at his slight awkwardness as nurses, domestics and physios all turned and had a good look!

He *was* particularly spectacular this morning.

Black jeans, black belt, a sheer white cotton shirt and Cuban-heeled boots. His hair was still damp and he had a silver loop in his ear. He looked drop-dead sexy.

'Will your brother be here yet?' Ross asked a while later.

'I would think so.' Annika glanced at her watch. 'Iosef is going to the airport to collect them.'

'So what's your mum got planned for you tonight?'

'Probably a big family reunion dinner, somewhere glitzy where the press can see us all smiling and laughing.'

'I'll give it a miss.' Ross gave her a wink. 'But thanks for the invite.'

'There was no invite.' Annika shot him a short smile back. 'You're a bad influence, remember?'

It was a busy morning, made busier because it was her last day on the ward and time for her end-of-rotation assessment.

'Well done.' Heather Jameson ticked all the boxes this time. In the last few weeks, though it had been hard at home, Annika had made work her solace, had put her head down, or sometimes up, had smiled when she didn't really feel like it and had been rewarded in a way she had never expected. 'I know you've had a difficult time personally, and that it took you a bit of time to settle, but you have. The staff are all delighted with you.'

'I've liked working on the children's ward,' Annika said. 'I never thought I would, but I truly have.'

'What do you like about it?'

'It's honest,' Annika said. 'The children cry and they laugh and they don't pretend to be happy.' She gave a small smile. 'They forgive you if you are not happy too,' Annika said, 'and so long as you are kind, they don't mind if you are quiet.'

'You've got Maternity next,' Heather said, and blinked when Annika rolled her eyes.

'You might like it—remember you weren't looking forward to Paeds?'

'I think I am too stoic to be sympathetic,' Annika said, 'but of course I will be. Now I know where I'm going.'

It was things like that that set her apart.

There was still an aloofness, a hard edge that bewildered Heather, but, yes, Annika was intriguing.

'Do you think Paediatrics is where you might specialise?' Heather said.

'No,' Annika said. 'I've decided what I want to do.'

'And?'

'Geriatrics or palliative care.' Annika smiled at Heather's slight frown. 'It has everything the children's ward has and a lot of wisdom too. I guess as you near the end of your life the mask slips away and you can be honest again.'

'You did very well in your geriatric rotation.'

'I thought it was because nursing was new,' Annika admitted. 'I thought the gloss had worn off over the last eighteen months or so. But now I realise nothing was ever as good as my time there, because geriatrics is the area of nursing where I belong.'

She thought of Elsie.

Of a white chocolate box filled with mousse and raspberries—and that nothing could taste so perfect, so why bother searching?

Idle chatter had come easily with Elsie and the oldies, and silence had been easy too.

'I want to qualify,' Annika explained. 'I want to get through the next year. I am not looking forward to Maternity, nor to working in Theatre, but I will do my best, and when I get my qualification I have decided that I would like to specialize in aged care.'

Oh, it wasn't as exciting as Emergency, or as impressive sounding as Paediatrics or ICU—but it was, Annika realised, an area of nursing she loved. She had been searching for something and had found it—so quickly, that she hadn't recognised it at first.

It was the care Annie had shown her father that had first drawn her into nursing—the shifts at the nursing home that had sustained her.

She liked old people.

For the most part they accepted her.

It was very hard to explain, but she tried.

'Those extra shifts that I did in the nursing home,' Annika admitted, 'they were busy, and it was hard work, but...' Still she could not explain. 'I like the miserable ones, the angry ones, the funny ones, even those I don't like, I like... They teach me, and I can help them just by stopping to listen, by making sure they have a chance to talk, or making sure they are clean and comfortable. It's a different sort of nursing.'

And Heather looked at a very neat, very well turned out, sometimes matter-of-fact, often awkward but always kind nurse, and realised that Geriatrics would be very lucky to have her. To be old, to have someone practical tend to the practical and then to have the glimpse of her warmth–well, they would be lucky to have her and also she would be lucky to have them.

She needed a few golden oldies bolstering her up, mothering her, gently teasing her, showing her how things could be done, how life could be funny even when it didn't feel it. It might just bring a more regular smile to those guarded lips.

'You'll be wonderful.'

It was the first compliment Annika had truly accepted.

'Thank you.'

'But you have to get through the next year.'

'I will,' Annika said. 'Now I know where I'm heading.'

'Right, you'd better get off for lunch.'

Was it already lunchtime?

Annika dashed into the changing room, opened her locker and ran a brush through her hair and then tied it back into its ponytail. She added some lip-gloss and went to squirt on some perfume—but remembered it was forbidden on the children's ward.

She couldn't wait to see Levander. Last time it had been so stressful, but with Aleksi improving there was much to celebrate, and she was looking forward to seeing Millie too, and little Sashar.

She dashed down the corridor and saw Ross,

standing talking to some relatives, and he caught her eye, gave her that smile, and it was as if he was waiting for her, had always been waiting patiently for her.

'Levander.' She hugged her brother when she reached Aleksi's room. It was so good to see him looking well and happy, and Sashar came to her easily. Millie was talking to Annie, who was holding Rebecca.

All the family were together, yet still her mother was not happy, still she could not just relax and enjoy it. She was talking in Russian, even though neither Millie nor Annie understood, telling her children her restaurant of choice for the Kolovsky dinner tonight.

'The hairdresser is at five, Annika.' Nina still spoke in Russian. 'Make sure that you come straight home.

'I'll come too.'

Annika frowned as Annie, for the first time in living memory, volunteered for a non-essential hour at the Kolovsky family home.

'If Iosef takes Rebecca home, I can hang around here and you can give me a lift.'

Annika looked to Iosef, who nodded.

'Hey!' Annika turned to Aleksi and kissed him. His face was pale and it worried her. 'Any better?'

'I'm fine,' Aleksi said, because he said the same each day. He was so tough, so removed from everyone, and so loathing this prolonged invasion of his privacy.

'You'll be home soon.'

'Nope!' A thin smile dusted his pale features. 'I'm sick of bloody family...' He turned to his PA who was there, a large, kind woman, always calm and unruffled, and whispered in her ear. 'Tell them, Kate.'

'Your brother's off to recover at a small island in the West Indies.'

'Very nice.' Annika smiled.

'I'm going into hiding,' Aleksi explained, with just a hint of a wink. That dangerous smile, Annika saw with relief, was starting to return.

'I refuse to be photographed like this—it will ruin my reputation.'

'It's irreparable!' Annika joked, and yet she was worried for him—more worried than he would want her to be, more worried than she could show. She would talk to Kate later–check out as best she could the details of his rehabilitation.

'Come and visit?' Aleksi said, but Annika shook her head.

'I can't. I'm going to Spain for my honeymoon,' Annika said, enjoying her brother's look of confusion.

The door opened, and Nina frowned as a forbidden doctor walked in.

'Family.' Nina said it like a curse. 'Family only.'

'Ross is family,' Annika said. 'Or rather he's about to be.'

She swallowed as the celebrant walked in behind Ross.

'Mrs Kolovsky.' Ross's voice was neither nervous nor wavering as the relatives he had been talking to in the corridor came in—*his* relatives, all happily in on the plan. 'Annika and I want no fuss, but we do want everyone we love present.'

She felt Aleksi's hand squeeze hers, saw Levander smile, and Iosef too. She was scared to see her mother's reaction, so she looked at Ross instead.

It was the teeniest, tiniest of weddings. But she was getting stronger and, with or without Ross, she would make it.

But as he took her hand and slipped on a heavy silver ring she knew that with Ross beside her she would get there sooner.

'By the power vested in me, I pronounce you man and wife.'

He kissed her, a slow, tender kiss that was patient and loving, and then he pulled her back and smiled.

The same smile that had kept her guessing all this time and would keep her guessing for years to come.

'I love you.' It was the first time she had ever said it, Annika realised. He had married her without the confirmation of those three little words.

'I always knew that one day you would,' Ross said. 'What's not to love?'

He made her stomach curl; he made her want to smile. There was excitement from just looking at him, and she wanted to look at him for ever, but for now there was duty.

'We would love to be there tonight,' Annika said to her mother's rigid face. 'Just for a little while.'

For her mother she would face the cameras and allow it to be revealed in the newspapers tomorrow that the Kolovsky heiress was married. She would smile, and she would have her hair done and wear a fabulous dress, but it would be one of her choosing.

'And I would like it if Ross's family could join in the celebration.'

'Of course...' Nina choked.

'Look after her,' Iosef said to Ross.

'I intend to.'

And Iosef could see his wife's tears, and understood all that she had been trying to say to him these past weeks.

His spoiled, lightweight, brat of a little sister was actually a woman of whom he should be proud—and he told her so.

'I am so proud of you.'

She had needed to hear it, and she smiled back at her brother and her sister-in-law, and then to Levander and Millie—and it dawned on her then.

They were all survivors.

Survivors who were busy pulling their own oars, rather than being dragged down—but how much easier it would be now if they pulled together.

There was only one who was still going it alone.

'Aleksi.' She smiled to her brother. 'I was going to speak to the nurse in charge, see if maybe we could come back here after dinner...' And then, much to her mother's annoyance, she changed the plans again. 'Or we could ring the restaurant and eat here.'

Aleksi wouldn't hear of it. 'Go out,' he said, and then gestured to his infusion. 'I'll be knocked out by seven anyway.'

He was, Annika realised, still rowing all by himself.

'Congratulations,' Aleksi said, and kissed his sister.

'The last single Kolovsky,' Annika teased. 'And still the Kolovsky wedding gown has not been worn.'

'It never will be, then.' He shook his new brother-in-law's hand. 'Take care of her.'

'He already has,' Annika said.

Yes, the tiniest of weddings—and still duty called.

But sometimes duty was a pleasure too.

They walked back down the corridor, laughing and chatting. A nurse and a doctor returning from their lunch break.

The ward was nice and quiet, darkened for the afternoon's quiet time, but Caroline wasn't best pleased. She was talking to Heather Jameson and was stern in her greeting to her student. Good report or not, it was inexcusable to be thirty minutes late back from lunch without good reason.

'Annika, it's forty-five minutes for lunch. I know your brother just arrived, but...'

'I am sorry,' Annika said. 'I was at Security; I had to pick up my new ID.'

Lifting up her lanyard, she offered it to Caroline.

'Well, next time...' Her voice trailed off. 'Annika Wyatt?'

Her neck almost snapped as she turned to Ross, then back to Annika.

'We just got married,' Annika explained, as if that was what people always did in their lunch break.

It seemed the strangest way to spend your wedding day, and no one but the two of them would understand, but there was freedom, real freedom, as she excused herself from the little gathering, smiled to her husband and colleagues, and did what she had fought so hard and for so long to do.

She started to live life her way.

MEDICAL™

Large Print

Titles for the next six months...

January

DARE SHE DATE THE DREAMY DOC?	Sarah Morgan
DR DROP-DEAD GORGEOUS	Emily Forbes
HER BROODING ITALIAN SURGEON	Fiona Lowe
A FATHER FOR BABY ROSE	Margaret Barker
NEUROSURGEON...AND MUM!	Kate Hardy
WEDDING IN DARLING DOWNS	Leah Martyn

February

WISHING FOR A MIRACLE	Alison Roberts
THE MARRY-ME WISH	Alison Roberts
PRINCE CHARMING OF HARLEY STREET	Anne Fraser
THE HEART DOCTOR AND THE BABY	Lynne Marshall
THE SECRET DOCTOR	Joanna Neil
THE DOCTOR'S DOUBLE TROUBLE	Lucy Clark

March

DATING THE MILLIONAIRE DOCTOR	Marion Lennox
ALESSANDRO AND THE CHEERY NANNY	Amy Andrews
VALENTINO'S PREGNANCY BOMBSHELL	Amy Andrews
A KNIGHT FOR NURSE HART	Laura Iding
A NURSE TO TAME THE PLAYBOY	Maggie Kingsley
VILLAGE MIDWIFE, BLUSHING BRIDE	Gill Sanderson

MILLS & BOON®

MEDICAL™

Large Print

April

BACHELOR OF THE BABY WARD	Meredith Webber
FAIRYTALE ON THE CHILDREN'S WARD	Meredith Webber
PLAYBOY UNDER THE MISTLETOE	Joanna Neil
OFFICER, SURGEON…GENTLEMAN!	Janice Lynn
MIDWIFE IN THE FAMILY WAY	Fiona McArthur
THEIR MARRIAGE MIRACLE	Sue MacKay

May

DR ZINETTI'S SNOWKISSED BRIDE	Sarah Morgan
THE CHRISTMAS BABY BUMP	Lynne Marshall
CHRISTMAS IN BLUEBELL COVE	Abigail Gordon
THE VILLAGE NURSE'S HAPPY-EVER-AFTER	Abigail Gordon
THE MOST MAGICAL GIFT OF ALL	Fiona Lowe
CHRISTMAS MIRACLE: A FAMILY	Dianne Drake

June

ST PIRAN'S: THE WEDDING OF THE YEAR	Caroline Anderson
ST PIRAN'S: RESCUING PREGNANT CINDERELLA	Carol Marinelli
A CHRISTMAS KNIGHT	Kate Hardy
THE NURSE WHO SAVED CHRISTMAS	Janice Lynn
THE MIDWIFE'S CHRISTMAS MIRACLE	Jennifer Taylor
THE DOCTOR'S SOCIETY SWEETHEART	Lucy Clark

MILLS & BOON

Discover Pure Reading Pleasure with

Visit the Mills & Boon website for all the latest in romance

Buy all the latest releases, backlist and eBooks

Join our community and chat to authors and other readers

Win with our fantastic online competitions

Tell us what you think by signing up to our reader panel

Find out more about our authors and their books

Free online reads from your favourite authors

Sign up for our free monthly eNewsletter

Rate and review books with our star system

www.millsandboon.co.uk

 Follow us at twitter.com/millsandboonuk

 Become a fan at facebook.com/romancehq